NOT JUST US

BY VICTORIA WARREN JACKSON

Can You Feel Me? Intimate Poetry

Untraditional Love In The Dark

Not Just Us

Victoria Warren Jackson

Not Just Us

A Novel

FAVIC PRESS

PUBLISHING COMPANY

FLORIDA

Published in the United States by Favic Press, Florida.

Publisher's Cataloging-in-Publication
(Provided by Quality Books, Inc.)

Jackson, Victoria Warren.
    Not just us / Victoria Warren Jackson.
    p. cm.
    LCCN 2010940104
    ISBN-13: 9780970742650
    ISBN-10: 0970742657

    1. HIV-positive women--Fiction. 2. Sisters--Fiction.
I. Title.

PS3573.A77947N68 2011   813'.54
                    QBI10-600243

This book is dedicated to my mother, Fannie Lindsey.

ACKNOWLEDGEMENTS

I thank God for giving me the ability to write. There was a time when I had given up on writing, but God had another plan for me.

To my husband, Wayne, for teaching me how to enjoy life, I love you.

To my mother for her wisdom, you helped to develop my passion for writing.

To my father for unconditional support, our family wouldn't be the same without you.

To my sisters for being a source of strength, it's nice to have my sisters in my corner.

To all of my readers who take the time to read my books, thank you.

Chapter One

There are some instances in life when we have no control over our own lives or destinations. However, the majority of the time, we write our own life story. Once the ball is in motion, only unbelievable faith will stop it from rolling.

Like most adults, we wait until our youth is gone to reflect on mistakes. It is a bittersweet transition. The bitter comes later after it is too late to change the past. Take dating for example. Dating is different as we get older. We become wiser and more reluctant to unprotected sex. A woman may contract Herpes in her youth but never pay attention to the consequences until she gets married and gives birth to a handicap child.

Another example of a bittersweet transition is body weight. As children, we may overeat for most of our lives. Finally when we reach adulthood, the fat cells have already developed. We then spend the remainder of our lives struggling to shed unwanted pounds. We think to ourselves, "If only I had known fat cells develop during childhood, I would have eaten more fruits and vegetables and less sweets."

You can be the strongest of individuals, but a day will come when problems enter your life, which cause "you to break". This is serious. Have you ever found yourself holding a conversation with someone, and they appear to be weird or strange? This is a person who has either had a nervous breakdown or is on the verge of having a nervous breakdown.

One day the stress level may become so high, you have no other choice but to surrender all to a Higher Power. Once upon a time in my life, I would call on Jesus to rescue me. I soon realized I was only calling Him when I was down, needy, or in trouble. I am somewhat of a religious person. I am not a fanatic. I do not push my beliefs off on other people. I am a quiet type of believer.

My religion is not a loud, look at me form of religion. It is private. I get weak and angry if the wrong buttons are pushed. I must admit; I do have a problem with getting to occupied with my own daily lifestyle and ultimately letting my spiritual life get shaky.

Anyway, no matter what the cause of the choices I make today or have made yesterday, I am still here in this body mourning. I am to old to be innocent and to young to be senile. I am a woman floating around in this world waiting for something wonderful to finally happen to me. When I was a teenager, I set goals for myself. I thought I would someday meet a man, get married, have a big home, and have some kids. A career would come later.

Well, here's to dreams. None of those things came true for me. Instead, I have worked my butt off going to school all of my life with a small paycheck to show for all my efforts. People working on a sex hotline can make more money than I make in a week. It is a shame I tell you. These thoughts constantly cross my mind, which leads to my reason for being sick and tired of being sick and tired. No, this is not a play on words. I meant exactly what I said. Besides, why can't I throw some dirt in the game? Everyone else does, and they get away with it.

Tonight, tonight, tonight. I want to fly away tonight. I do not want to be in an airplane. My spirit is low, and I want to fly away home. This is a metaphor meaning I want to be anywhere else besides where I am right now.

I do believe I will go to heaven when I die. People are talking so much about Jesus returning soon. I pray He makes it back before I go insane.

If Jesus does not return soon, I will be forced to watch my sister, whose name is Desiree, die from the AIDS virus or AIDS-related complications. Every family will experience the AIDS epidemic, but not mine, so I thought.

As kids, my sister and I grew up playing together and enjoying nice gifts from our mother. The only difference between my sister and I was she got more gifts because she is older.

I never truly cared because she has always

been my role model. I did not mind accepting her hand-me-downs. She had great taste in clothes. She also took really good care of her clothes. They looked almost new when I got them.

While the memories replay in my head, the days I spent watching my sister puzzle me. Mature and anxious are words to describe my sister as she became a curious teenager who wanted to date. The only problem was my mother felt it was way too soon. My mother expected my sister to wait until she was eighteen-years-old before dating just in case she got pregnant. My mother is from the Deep South. Parents raised in the Deep South have old-fashioned values.

My sister wanted to date. My mother refused to accept her decision. This caused the biggest war in all history. I call it war because things were never the same in our home after they started to argue about everything. My sister totally rebelled against my mother. My mother did everything she could to protect my sister from the world, but they never seemed to understand each other. I cannot remember a pleasant day shared between the two of them after my mother caught my sister skipping school to be with a boyfriend. They have been at war ever since that dreaded day.

Who is to blame? I really do hate to take sides. They both need to be more humble if you ask me. They are both quite hot-tempered and quick with words. My mother throws her opinions around, and my sister tends to retaliate. Although I have tried to convince my sister to let go of her anger, she ignores me and walks away. Pride is a strong emotion, especially when it controls a person.

Sometimes, it does not make a difference if a child gets the best of everything from their parents. I have known kids who go astray regardless of what their parents give them. Who knows what their minds are telling them? Sadly enough, kids do not understand the consequences of their rebellion. Many learn their lesson to late.

Some kids are able to make it, and become productive citizens. Women, for example, who have lived troubled lives and become role models, cry in their hotel rooms late at night. The world admires them, but they hate or dislike themselves. They are unable to release the past. The past harasses them like a filthy secret. Memories of the past can cause a woman to kill herself. The mirror may display a well-dressed, successful woman. Through her eyes, she sees a worthless, abused, little girl with low self-esteem.

We all make mistakes while we are young. Most of us refuse to think about our past because it is way to painful for us. When we are young, we fail to take advice from adults because we think we know it all. We appoint ourselves to be adults when really we are still inexperienced about life.

The only problem with being a "self-appointed adult" is the decision to commit adult acts. Adults have considerable difficulties being an adult. There is no way a child can handle the pressures of being an adult. Everything comes in due season. A child is not equipped mentally to handle adult situations.

I am not an expert on life. I have my skeletons to prove it. However, I can share a bit of knowledge every now and then, anticipating some young soul will listen and take heed. It is a nasty world we live in. People are for themselves and themselves only. If you get in their way, they will crush you! When you are young, you are innocent to these things, unless you cross over into the shoes of an adult.

Young ladies in particular must be ever so careful as to the decisions they make in life. One bad decision today can ruin your life forever! Good decisions will bring good results. Bad decisions will bring misery. My grandmother always told me, "Be sure your sins will find you out." There is nowhere to hide if you are stuck on being stupid, no way to hide, nowhere to hide. This is the reality of it all if you are determined to be rebellious. Do the right thing.

When her hormones started to flair, my sister went against all of the values she had learned at home. The heat was much to strong for her to say "no". During her ninth-grade year in high school, she gave her virginity to Glover, the most popular boy in school. All the young ladies wanted to be seen with Glover. He dressed nice. He could dance. He was on the football team. His mother bought him expensive sneakers to match all of his outfits. He had a cellular phone. He drove his mother's car to school several days a week. He was voted as being the *Most Popular* boy in the entire school.

Today, seventeen years later, he is a bum! A friend of mine was gossiping about him a couple of days ago. Glover does not have a job; he still lives home with "mommy", and he has four children with four different women. "Mommy" never cut the umbilical cord.

Glover has managed to keep his good looks and his cocky attitude. He still thinks he is back in high school when all the young ladies had a crush on him. He better wake up. His fifteen minutes of fame is finished.

My sister went crazy over Glover whenever she saw him at school. Infatuation had its' way with my sister. Her secret is my secret. She does not realize I know the first time she had sex. I snuck and read about it in her diary. The diary read, "We did it on the P.E. field in the dug-out." She described the act as being painful. She even described how she cried. I was young when I read her diary. I got scared and threw the diary underneath her bed. I never told a soul.

That was the kind of relationship my sister and I had. I thought I was doing her a favor by keeping her promiscuous behavior a secret from our mother.

My sister and Glover did not date for very long

after they had sex. He was a popular young man in school. He could have any girl in the school. He did not need my sister anymore. He had gotten what he wanted.

Glover never officially broke-up with Desiree. He just started avoiding her. Whenever she would see him in the hallways, he would go in the opposite direction or pretend as though he did not see her. She did confront him. Glover promised to meet her at lunchtime to talk about their relationship. Desiree waited by the big oak tree in front of the school for the entire lunch period. Glover did not keep his word. After the last bell rang, Desiree walked inside of the building heading to her third period class. Upstairs, near the Graphic Arts Class, she saw Glover with Sebrinna Walker. They were holding hands and giggling.

Desiree called Glover's name. He looked around, saw her, and then pressed through the crowd of students. Desiree was left standing there wanting Glover to return.

Glover promised Desiree he would not tell anyone about having sex with her. He lied. The next day after they "did it" when Desiree arrived to school, Carol approached her with a big grin on her face. She told my sister what Glover had told some of his friends. Carol was dating Glover's best friend. Desiree was going to go looking for Glover. She was hurt because he betrayed her trust.

She saw him after the first block. He was coming down the stairs by the Attendance Office wearing a pair of blue jeans and a t-shirt. He had his arms stretched in the air while yawning with his mouth wide open. Desiree pulled him to the side.

"You told them," Desiree said.

"Not now, Desiree. I am tired. I got home late last night," Glover replied.

"I don't care. Why did you tell them?"

"I only told Roy. He is my best friend."

"You promised you wouldn't tell anybody. I am so embarrassed."

"For what? You are my girlfriend."

"You make me sick. That's all you wanted from me. Everybody will be talking about me."

"The bell is about to ring. I will talk to you later."

Glover walked away. His yawn turned into a big smile. He had conquered. His friends were all congratulating him while my sister was depressed. Her virginity was gone forever.

Desiree had a best friend whom she spent hours talking to on the telephone. I would listen in on her phone conversations. Desiree trusted me. She knew I would not tell our mother anything.

I know so many secrets about my sister. After she and Glover stopped dating, she dated other boys from school. She wanted to make Glover jealous, not knowing he cared less about anything she did.

In my heart, I take some responsibility for my sister's predicament. I could have protected her. The boys sneaking in her window, the excuses to go to her friend's house, reasons for working late, all of her lies served their purpose. She was giving it up more than a prostitute on the boulevard. Her lies have all come back to haunt her. She is now infected with HIV. I should have told my mother what I knew. Maybe my mother could have stopped Desiree.

My sister suspected she was sick even before the doctor told her about the positive HIV test results. She had contracted venereal disease after venereal disease. Why she trusted men so much I will never know. She had condoms. Her doctor gave her a bag of condoms. She just did not use them, silly girl. When pleasure pushed her buttons, she melted like cheese.

The finest man in town infected Desiree with HIV. When they met, he was dressed nice, smelling nice, and carrying a lot of cash. Not only was he driving a fancy car, he had on expensive jewelry. If I were Desiree, I would have checked his police record before getting involved with him.

Men have hurt me, and I do not trust them. These days, men do not come wrapped in shimmery packages unless they have won the lottery or are selling drugs. Oh yes, they may get lucky enough to find a decent paying job. If the truth must be told, then let me tell it. Women are making the dollars, and men are trying to compete.

All across America, men are playing games. Most of them have no jobs, play basketball at lunchtime, and scout the neighborhood for women walking to the bus stop. They lie about being on a professional sports team be it football or basketball. When confronted about making money, they insist their manager is getting work for them. I have heard this stupid line from many men. One man told me he was going overseas to play basketball. Excuse me for laughing. The man was in his late twenties when I met him, and he was not in good shape. He wore his gold gym shorts hanging down on his big butt. His shirt could not hide his sloppy stomach. And his legs did not appear to be muscular. The only thing going for him was his cute face.

I have to tell the truth. I was attracted to him for some reason. He could make me laugh. His name is James.

I did give James my phone number. He called, and we went on a couple of dates. And I did have sex with him. I think both of us were looking for the same thing, friendship. Our friendship was unusual. We had sex everywhere. I recall us getting busy in an abandoned car parked in his neighborhood. I knew then our friendship was way to dangerous for me. I told him goodbye that night and did not accept another phone call from him again.

I am not worried. I always used protection with James. He could have had a girlfriend. I did not ask him if he was sleeping with anyone else. We had an understanding. We both understood our relationship would not go beyond being anything more than a "sexual friendship".

The suave man who swept my sister off her feet had a cute face like James. He appeared to be nice, but he was really a low-life drug dealer. I knew something was "stank in his tank". He had too much money to be so young. He was not an entertainer because I had never seen his face on any billboard or any album.

I thought he would not be in her life for very long. Desiree has a history of indulging with many men. She once told me, "I want exactly what they want."

Now, her tune has changed. She has kids to worry about. Who will get her kids after she is gone? I will gladly do whatever I can to raise them. I know it may be tough, but I will do it for my sister's sake. It would not be right to give the kids to the state.

I sit and wonder when Desiree's day will come to say goodbye to us all. Will it be in five years? Will she live as long as thirteen years? What will become of our family? We are all suffering along with Desiree. From the positive test results to the constant sick days, we have stood by her side.

Family has to stick together.

My sister resented her family in the past. She thought we were only trying to get in her business, or tell her what to do. More than anything else, my mother was trying to prevent her from this terrible fate.

It is ripping me apart. Every glance into her eyes hurts me. I refuse to accept the fact she will not be around. She has always been here. Someday, she will be gone to another place. And I will not be able to call her on the telephone or go shopping with her. My big sister will be in the cemetery. Her children will lose their mother, and I will lose a life-long friend.

Life is so unfair to us all. If Adam and Eve had not eaten from the Tree of Life, we could all live forever. Things would be better. I cannot bear the thought of Desiree leaving me. Who will I go to with my problems?

In the spur of the moment, I could race to a payphone to tell Desiree what was going on at my job. She never turned me away. She would listen, and tell me to calm down. Her not being around for me will place a void in my life.

Why do situations of our youth haunt us in adulthood even after we change our life? My sister did change. She even found a job. She got a new car and started taking care of her kids. She has struggled to become a better person. Even when she was down-and-out, I saw the good in her.

Death is promised to us all. It comes when we least expect it. When someone has AIDS, most of the guesswork is alleviated. When, and if, the virus finally destroys the immune system, the doctors can pretty much determine when the person will die.

Desiree is in the early stages of HIV. She appears to be normal on the outside. No one will ever know she is infected with HIV unless she tells them. She could even continue dating if she chooses to do so. My sister has a heart. At least I can give her credit for not intentionally dating men to spread the virus.

My sister has no intention of infecting anyone else with the virus. The man in her life, today, was infected by my sister. She did not know she had the virus when they started dating. She did not know her ex-boyfriend had given her HIV. Her new boyfriend has to pay the ultimate price for not wearing a condom. Ironically enough, he has learned to deal with his fate. He has vowed to stay with Desiree. He understands she was not aware the virus was in her system. She did not purposely infect him.

A woman at my job was talking about AIDS. She is not very educated, but her statement made a valid point. She said, "The smoothest talking men are carrying a bomb in their penis. When it explodes, don't let it be in you!"

We all have a choice. When having sex, it is best to use protection. Be safe rather than sorry. One minute of pleasure is not worth a lifetime of pain.

Chapter Two

Tonight is the first time in months Desiree and I have held a woman-to-woman conversation. Even though we are both adults, and have been adults for many years, we do our best to respect each other's feelings. We do this by discussing simple topics like television shows or why our favorite sports team never wins a game. If one of us has something on our mind, and would like to share with the other, then we talk openly. We have always tried to remain respectful and not cross the line.

As I sit at my computer typing an assignment

for class, my telephone rings. I am not sure who is calling me, so I answer it on the first ring. I do not want my boyfriend, Patrick, to wake up. Although only one man calls my house, besides my boyfriend, this could be the night; Elroy decides to give me a call.

Elroy is an ex-boyfriend. We talk occasionally. He will always have a special place in my heart. He calls me once in a while to say hello.

After answering the telephone, I realize it is Desiree speaking in a low pitch. "Shanna, are you up?" she asks me.

"Yes. I am trying to finish my project for Humanities Class. I have to turn it in tomorrow morning at 8:00 a.m. I only have to type the Bibliography Page. I also have an exam in the morning. Lucky me."

"You should be so proud of yourself. At least one of us did something with our life."

"Desiree, you did something with your life. You may not have chosen to attend college, but you have two beautiful children. At least you have been married. You even have a nice man in your life that cares about you and your children. Here

I am, an unmarried woman with no children and a small bank account," I finish my sentence then laugh.

"Well, keep up the good work. You know you are the apple of mama's eye."

"I can't tell. Just yesterday I left her house upset because she told me my butt is to big. I can't help it if I have a big butt. I can't cut it off. I just want to know where it came from."

"Shanna, do not go into that phase again. Even if you do not know who your father is, you are still doing fine."

"I want to get to know him. I want to know if I resemble him. Did I get my figure from his side of the family? Is he a dark-skinned man or a bright-skinned man? Who are my paternal relatives? I want to know. You can't fault me for being curious."

Desiree listens as I rant-and-rave on and on about a father whom I do not know and will probably never get to meet. Once a psychic told me my father is Creole. The psychic could have been lying to me. She could not tell me if I am ever going to get married. If she is a psychic, why couldn't she answer my question about marriage?

I do not speak with an accent. No one in my family speaks with an accent. Off hand, I am not familiar with anyone in this town who speaks with an accent. The psychic has to be wrong. My mother has never mentioned going to New Orleans or outside the United States for vacation.

People from New Orleans have an accent. Some people from Caribbean Islands have an accent. There is nothing wrong with having an accent. I am only suggesting every culture has unique words they use, which are unfamiliar to other cultures. I see nothing wrong with speaking differently. That's what makes the human race so beautiful. We are all different, but similar in so many ways.

My grandmother always told me, "What's in the dark will come to the light." As a child, I never understood what this phrase meant. As a teenager, I still did not understand the phrase. Today, as a twenty-two-year-old woman, I understand it perfectly well. Although my mother still insists my sister and I have the same father, I know she is lying.

To be honest, I have known for many years about the truth. No one has ever come to me and confirmed my suspicions, but my gut feeling tells me all I need to know. I have watched my sister with her so-called good hair, pointy noise, and brown eyes. She looks exactly like the man who claims to be our father.

Me, on the other hand, I have to get my hair permed once a month. If I go without a perm, I would look like a woman from the bushes of Africa. My hair situation is not the only dead giveaway. I have nappy hair, a wide nose, dark-brown eyes, and a big butt. My nose, butt, and facial features say it all. My features are more like a woman from New Orleans. There is something mysterious about my features. My sister and I have different complexions. My complexion is similar to coffee with two tablespoons of cream.

People from New Orleans have exotic features. This is because slaves from Haiti gave birth to babies fathered by French gentlemen. New Orleans has a rich history of breeding babies. The act of breeding babies in New Orleans started during slavery with the freed slaves and the men who "kept" them as mistresses. My mother could have visited New Orleans for Mardi Gras. Maybe this is when or where she met my father.

There is no way to convince me otherwise. Desiree and I do not have the same father. One plus one will always equal two. My mother has bright skin. The man who claims to be my father has bright skin. My sister has bright skin. My skin is darker than the three of them put together.

My mother does not know how I feel about my real father. She will probably hold on to her lie forever, and carry it with her to the grave. I think it is so unfair to me. I deserve to know. Even if she did not get along with my biological father, or he decided he does not want me, still tell me the truth. Why not let me know who my real father is? I know women make mistakes in their life. I can testify to this. I know my mother was not perfect.

I would accept the fact she dated him for a couple of months and got pregnant. Even if they danced together on Bourbon Street in New Orleans during Mardi Gras then took it further with no promises of commitment, I would accept this as well. My father could have decided fatherhood was not for him at the time. Maybe he had a wife at home. I can deal with being the product of a one-night stand.

Those things are irrelevant. At this moment, I can deal with almost anything except a lie.

I don't understand why my mother has and still holds to her lie. Is she afraid I will hate her? I could never hate the woman who gave me life and took care of me all of my life. Yes, I would be a little angry, but I would eventually get over the anger. I need to know who this secret man is. I am no longer a child, and I believe my mother owes me more than "silence". My sister tells me to leave well enough alone. She thinks my mother will never speak to me again if I mention this topic to her. I don't want to lose my relationship with my mother, so I have to hold my feelings inside.

I am a firm believer all children deserve to know who their biological father is. If he chooses not to take part in his child's life, let it be on his conscience. A mother should never keep a child away from their father to seek revenge or make him suffer.

The child pays in the end. I am not dysfunctional. There are those who will say their life went wrong because they felt unwanted by their father. It does happen everyday.

As our telephone conversation continues,

Desiree and I start talking about life and how we are all destined before we are ever born.

"Shanna, let go. One day you will know the truth. Until then what can you do besides worry yourself to death over the unknown?"

"It's easy for you to say stop worrying. You know who your father is. You know where you came from and who your relatives are. I know nothing. It does hurt as I grow older."

"Leave it in God's Hands, Shanna. Pray about it, and wait on God."

"I have been waiting. How much longer will I have to wait? I know God will come through when He is ready. God always comes right on time."

"Look at me. You have your health and strength. At least you can wake up in the morning and make plans for your future. I have to make plans for my funeral. It would be stupid for me to make long-term plans. Who knows how long I have to live? I have been thinking about my condition all day long. I can't eat. The only time I get peace is when I am asleep. This virus is driving me insane," Desiree tells me.

"I wish I knew what to say to you."

"Oh, don't worry, Shanna. I have learned to accept my situation. I will die from AIDS someday. I am continuing with my life, but it is so difficult. When I am gone, my children will be left behind. I hate the idea of leaving my kids behind. No one can love them like a mother. No one will love them unconditionally. No one will lay down their life for them like I would."

"I never thought this would happen in our family. I am doing my best to be strong for you. I have been keeping myself busy, so I will not have to think about HIV or AIDS. What would I ever do without you?" I ask Desiree.

"You have no other choice but to go on with your life, Shanna. You cannot stop living after I am gone. I pray you will care for my children as though you are their mother. Promise me you will not allow them to be separated. I want my children to stay together."

"You know I will take them in. I may not be the perfect person, but I can learn how to be a mother. I have to learn. I am their aunt."

"I trust you will keep your word. I know you will be a good mother. Whenever this virus kills me, and I go to a better place, I will be watching you all from heaven. On the other hand, I pray I live long enough to see my daughter grow up. If I can live to see her turn eighteen or nineteen-years-old, I will be satisfied. I don't want some slick talking man to come along and ruin her life. I want to protect her."

My sister and I remain in silence. I am doing everything I can to prevent myself from crying. My eyes are filled with tears. I have to be strong for Desiree.

I can hear the pain in my sister's voice. She has been more relaxed than ever since she was told she is HIV positive. In the beginning, she kept the news to herself. She did not want to tell us. She was not sure how we would react. I am the weakling in the family. The slightest bit of drama makes me almost have a nervous break down. I am glad Desiree trusted us enough to share her secret.

We are her family. She needs us. Some families would disown her or be embarrassed. We are not that kind of family.

I see my sister. I hear my sister. I can even feel my sister when I hug her. The idea of not being able to do any of these things would devastate me.

I sometimes wish I could lie down and die with her. I do not want her to travel this journey alone. I know she is afraid of death.

Lately, my sister tells me how she regrets not going to church very much. Personally, I think the church lives in your heart. Even if you are not in an actual church building, you can still glorify God every second of the day. Besides, God knows every detail about each of his creations, and He will definitely make each of us change if he sees fit. The wrath of God is the worst punishment for sin.

Some people go to church every Sunday. They will go to Wednesday Night Prayer Meeting, Jail House Missionary Work on Saturday, and they fast all day Friday. These same people think they are superior to others. There are those who are true Christians everyday of the week. Then there are those Christians who fake the walk and fake the talk.

I used to go to church a lot. As the years passed by, I stopped going so much. I got to busy with work and school. Last year, I took a leave of absence from my job as a regional manager for a

Tupperware company. I decided to attend school full-time to keep my mind occupied on days when I felt as though I was going "nuts".

When I was punching the clock six days a week, I spent every hour thinking about Desiree. I was afraid she would get sick, and I would not be able to leave work to help her. I had to weigh and balance my options. Family comes first in my life. There is nothing more important than family, not even the mighty dollar bill.

I want to spend as much time as possible with Desiree. I want her to be able to reach me at all times. My professors do not agree with students having cellular phones ringing during class, but I am an exception to the rule. I went to all of my professors when the semester started and explained my situation to them. I told them my sister is ill, and she has to be able to contact me if something goes wrong.

One of my professors was persistent about his rules and cellular phones. I did not want to go over his head to the department chairperson. I waited until the second week of class to talk with him again about my cellular phone.

I told him there is a possibility she may never call

during his class. I only wanted to get his permission to leave my cellular phone on during class. Eventually he gave in after the fourth week of class.

He was so mean whenever I spoke with him. He wanted me to accept his rules with no debate. I am a fighter. I refused to accept "no".

It is best to be nice even when someone else is being mean. My professor noticed I was not rude or disrespectful when I spoke to him. During all of our meetings, I remained polite and respectful. He told me, "The only reason I will give you permission to leave your cellular phone on in class is because you appear to be a nice person." I was shocked when he said that. This proves kindness goes a long way.

Regardless of what the outcome would have been, my cellular phone was staying on. And I was prepared to deal with the consequences. There is one thing I have learned in life. If you don't stand for something, you will fall for anything. I am a strong woman, and no one will push me around unless I am getting something from the deal.

See, in life, you have to pick and choose your battles. Some battles are not worth fighting. I did not want to battle with my professors.

They have something I want. I had to be kind to prevent conflict. I want to earn an "A" from all of my classes. The only way a professor will give a student an "A" in a course is if they like the student.

I can write a book describing how to be an "A" student. This is my own personal recipe for becoming an "A" student. It requires 20% studying, 5% perfect attendance, 15% class participation, 10% test taking, 7% kindness to your classmates, 5% pretending to enjoy the class, and 38% impressing the professor. This is a tried and true recipe. It works every time. If a student thinks they can study hard, pass the exams, complete all of the class assignments, and earn an "A" in the course, they are misleading themselves.

Professors like to see their students communicating. Professors value students who ask questions about lecture notes. The question does not have to be a thought-provoking question. It can be a simple gesture to let the professor know you are still awake.

Another aspect of being an "A" student is being phony with the professor. You have to make the professor believe you adore them and their teaching strategies. Students who earn "B's" instead of "A's" have not mastered the art of being phony with their professor.

It is so easy to convince a professor you adore them. Begin by acknowledging the professor whenever you enter the class. Always say, "Hello Professor." Then give them a warm smile. Before leaving class, say, "Goodbye Professor. Have a fabulous day." Send the professor an email once a week. In the email, discuss what you like about the class. Keep the email short and sweet. After every quiz or exam, be sure to ask the professor a question. Any question will suffice. Allow the professor to respond to your question. Flash the professor a big smile. Then say, "Thank you so much professor. I love this class."

I have a copy of my recipe in my notebook. I carry it with me to every class just in case I am having a bad day, and I am having trouble remembering how to be an "A" student.

Inside the classroom, I become an actress. The professor and the peers are my audience. I have to constantly remind myself to be the actress and not Shanna. My professors think I am a considerate person, which means my recipe is working.

I am not always kind. I can be a tough cookie

if pushed the wrong way. I guess walking through the fire and getting burnt has a way of making anyone tough. In addition to life's troubles, I am growing stronger as I deal with my sister's illness. Nothing in life comes before family besides God. Without family, I am nothing. When all the riches and gold fade away and friends are no more, family will still be here.

I am a daydreamer. I can hold a conversation while reflecting on another topic. I am speaking to Desiree on the telephone and reflecting on my experiences as a college student.

"Shanna, I better let you go. I am going to sleep. I will call you in the morning."

"Okay. Where are the kids?"

"They are asleep. I made them eat dinner then go to bed. I can't stand to hear their noise anymore. They have to be in bed by eight-thirty every night."

"Eight-thirty is to early. Let them watch television until nine. They are kids you know."

We laugh together. The only difference in our laugh today is the level of sincerity. Our laugh is real not forced.

After we say good-bye, I go into the bathroom and close the door. I place my hands over my eyes to catch my tears. My sister... My sister really does have HIV. It could have been me. I have not been a saint. I had unprotected sex with men. Why my sister got the virus instead of me is a mystery.

If I die, my family can cremate me, and pour my ashes in the sea. I do not have much to leave behind. I do not have any children. All of my earthly belongings can be donated to the Salvation Army.

My sister has so much to leave behind when she dies. Her most valued possessions will remain on Earth, her children.

I have said I would trade places with my sister if I could. On the other hand, I would not know how to walk around everyday knowing I have the HIV virus. I would probably focus on nothing else except death. Sure people live for ten or more years with the virus. It can be done. My only concern is the emotional stress. Stress would defeat my chances of ever living a normal life.

If a cure is not found for AIDS, my family will not be the first or the last family to lose a relative to this deadly virus.

CHAPTER THREE

I am probably the most superstitious person alive.
Most folks from the Deep South are superstitious.
We learn folktales from our parents who learned
them from their parents. Superstitions are passed
down from generation to generation.

Everybody carries a bit of superstition in their
blood. There are superstitions about black cats
crossing your path causing bad luck. Another
superstition is about cats having nine lives. I have
yet to see a cat resurrect from the dead. There are
superstitions about breaking a mirror. They say
you have ten years of bad luck if you break a mirror.

My grandmother used to tell me it is bad luck to sweep someone's feet with a broom. There is a superstition about pregnant women. They say a pregnant woman should never crave for a food while she is pregnant. She should go ahead, and eat the food. If she does not eat the food she is craving, she will supposedly "mark" her child. In elementary school, there was a little girl in my class by the name of Monica. Her birthmark is found in the center of her arm. My grandmother told me Monica's mother was having a craving while she was pregnant and scratched her stomach really hard. While scratching her stomach, she placed a "mark" on her unborn child's arm.

I do not know how true this superstition is. My grandmother tried to explain the concept for me. All superstitions have a bit of truth in them. They all come from someone who may have experienced them.

My bathroom is small. It is not fancy. I have a pink rug on the floor to match the shower curtains. The trashcan has pink flowers on it. The toilet is white. The medicine cabinet is gray. The tile on the floor is white. The tub is peach. My bathroom is not fit for a queen. It is only comfortable enough to suit my daily needs.

When I was around seven-years-old, I dreamt about living in a big mansion. The mansion was huge with thirteen bedrooms, five bathrooms, and a yard the size of a football field. My bathrooms in the mansion were all decorated with a Jacuzzi and a shower. All of the fixtures in the bathrooms were trimmed with gold. The towels were white with my initials embroidered on them.

I wanted to be famous. I wanted to own a mansion like royalty or rich people. I also imagined I would marry a rich man who would give me expensive diamonds for my neck and fingers. My young mind was not worldly enough to realize I was born to a middle-class mother who did not inherit any money from her ancestors.

Speaking of being rich, money could save Desiree. If I had lots of money, I would pay scientists to work around the clock to find a cure for AIDS.

Desiree always manages to make me cry. She does not do it intentionally. She has asked me not to be sad. I can't help it. She is my only sister.

I stand here facing the mirror, watching myself cry. The circles underneath my eyes are getting darker. The area between my eyebrows looks like a zigzag line. Signs of frustration invade my once flawless face. The more I look at myself in the mirror, the more I cry.

I turn the water on to wash my face. The water is cold. The water has to run for a few seconds before it gets warm. I stand here with my left hand held underneath the water waiting until it gets warm. The water is soft as it trickles through my fingers.

I am stronger than this. I can stay here in this bathroom all night crying like a baby, or I can finish my assignment. Staying here crying will not do me any good. I will not benefit in anyway. For the time being, Desiree is at home with her children. She is not in pain. Her kids will have their mother when they wake up in the morning. This is all I can ask for.

My class is not until tomorrow morning. If I stay here crying all night long, my assignment will be incomplete. The result will be a failing grade. Desiree wouldn't want me to fail my class.

Passing this class will place me one step closer to earning a degree. Failing this class will place me one step backwards.

As the water goes down the drain, I hear a loud sound. I turn the faucet to stop the water. The sound is coming from outside. I step into the bathtub to open the window in the bathroom.

I glance straight ahead. There in perfect view is a small sports car. The owner can't get it to start. He is pressing on the gas pedal causing the engine to roar. The car is not moving.

Pop-pop-pop comes from the engine. The car then moves a short distance and jumps. The owner presses the gas pedal a little more. An annoying rumble comes from the engine. This is ridiculous! The nerve of him. He should have done this earlier today. No one wants to listen to his engine at this time of night. He needs to call a tow truck to tow his car.

I watch on as a young man goes to the rear of the car. He waits for a signal then pushes the car forward. The car begins to move. The owner drives his car slowly to the corner and makes a right turn. The car is no longer in sight, but I can hear the engine making a growling sound.

I remain in the bathroom's window. As I suspected, he is returning. The car is barely moving. Maybe he needs a new battery. It could be his transmission.

He can leave his car in the middle of the road for all I care. My concern is his disrespect for his neighbors. My advice to him would be to park the car. Wait until morning comes to get it started. There are plenty of people in this area who have worked all day long and are tired. Eventually, someone will call the police on him.

My tears disappear. My thoughts of Desiree transform into anger for the man with the noisy car. People are so inconsiderate these days. They only care about themselves. He is determined to get his car started at any cost.

I have to study. I step from inside the bathtub onto the floor. I remove my bath towel from the rack to wipe my face. I replace it when my face is dry. Before leaving the bathroom, I turn off the lights.

I walk into the hallway. Patrick is already in bed asleep. I can see him stretched across the bed. His head is covered with a pillow. He is the strangest man. I told him not to cover his head with a pillow at night. He can suffocate.

I want to wake him. He is on cloud nine while I am here suffering. This happens way to often in homes. It is easy to live in the same home with a person and be lonely. Patrick is here physically, but he is not here mentally. Patrick has grown accustomed to not communicating with me. He does not sit down with me to comfort me. I agree both parties have to put forth effort to strengthen communication in a relationship. However, it is quite difficult to communicate with a self-absorbed man. The concept of communication is too broad for him to comprehend.

I will join him soon. In the middle of the night, I plan to elbow him in the back. This is my way of getting revenge. I will act as though I am unaware of what I did. He will think my elbowing him is accidental.

I have to type a Bibliography Page. I can do this in five minutes. I wrote my references on index cards. The index cards are numbered from one to ten. The information is alphabetized by author, volume, source, page number, and publisher.

I purchased a book to teach me how to do a research paper using the APA style. This is the most popular style for writing research papers. Initially, I went to the school's library to look for examples of research papers using the APA format. *The American Psychological Journal* has examples. I made copies of the research papers relating to my topic. There were so many examples in the journal. I did not have enough money to copy the entire journal.

I debated sticking the journal in my book bag to bring it home with me. I would have returned it after I finished getting what I needed. I am not a thief. I decided not to follow through because there is a security detector at the exit. The alarm sounds whenever a book or journal is removed from the library without being scanned.

It is quiet in the apartment. I can only concentrate when it is quiet. I have to be able to focus on what I am doing. I go directly to my computer. The monitor sits on a brown table with the computer to the side. The Screen Saver is red. The folders on the desktop are organized by title. My computer is not up-to-date, but it gets the job done.

I sit down in my chair and begin to type. My index cards are stacked neatly in a pile. I reach for card number one. After typing the information, I proceed to card number two, and then card three, and so on.

The light from the computer blares into my eyes. My eyes feel dry. The crying has made my eyelids feel heavy. I blink my eyes as I rush to finish my typing.

I am so grateful. My assignment is ready. Before exiting my document, I move the arrow to the top of the toolbar to click on File. This is where the print function is located. Within seconds of clicking on print, the lights on the printer begin to flash. The printer clicks to prepare for printing. The first page of the document appears. The other pages arrive next.

When the document is finished printing, I shut down my computer. I already have a black folder on my desk. My assignment will go in this folder. Black is a profound color. Professional documents should always be placed inside of black presentation folders. I want to impress my professor, so I spent a couple of extra dollars to purchase a black presentation folder.

I have to put three holes in my paper before placing it inside the black presentation folder. The three-hole puncher is in the drawer attached to the computer desk. I open the drawer to retrieve the three-hole puncher. I position my papers in the three-hole puncher then press down to form the holes. After removing the papers from inside of the three-hole puncher, I see the holes. I place the three-hole puncher back inside the drawer. Next, I place my research paper inside of the presentation folder.

I lay my assignment on the computer. I will put it in my book bag in the morning. My pep talk worked after all. I am glad I convinced myself to leave the bathroom to finish my assignment. I am done. Bed, here I come.

Chapter Four

The alarm clock goes off at six o'clock a.m. I have to force myself to get out of bed to turn it off. It is still dark outside. I peek through the vertical blinds in my bedroom. I can see a darkened sky with a handful of stars remaining from last night.

As I release the vertical blinds, I take a big stretch. My neck is sore. Patrick sleeps like a wild man. He takes most of the bed. I have to constantly fight for my space during the night.

I look over at Patrick who has not moved. I am sure he heard the alarm. He will stay here in the bed until I hit him, or start yelling at him. Sometimes, Patrick can be worse than a child.

I grab my robe from the side of the bed. I slide my arms into the sleeves while I look over at Patrick. I guess he wants me to shower first.

After getting into my robe, I pull it close to my body. It is cold in here. The air conditioner is set to sixty degrees. Depending on the weather, the air conditioner typically feels cooler before dawn. This makes the apartment colder than an icebox.

In the dark, I walk from the bedroom into the hallway and then into the bathroom. I switch on the bathroom's light. The sharp glare from the light hurts my eyes. I close my eyes then re-open them. This is my normal routine every morning. It takes my eyes at least fifteen minutes to get adjusted to light in the morning.

I wish class were cancelled. I want to stay here in my bed. I would sleep all day. Why can't I be rich? I wouldn't have to force myself to go to school. I would become an entrepreneur and open a daycare center.

We need more daycare centers. Working mothers should be able to work and not worry about their baby. It is so dangerous today. Mothers have to be careful when putting their baby in a daycare center. There are just to many freaks walking around.

I think the best person to care for a baby is the grandmother. A grandmother would never hurt their grandchild. Grandmothers learn parenting skills from their own children. They then put their expertise into practice with their grandchildren. A mother can rest assured her baby is safe with the grandmother.

It is not always a wise idea to allow family members to babysit. You may trust all of your family members, but this does not qualify them to be a good babysitter.

Behind closed doors, people are capable of doing anything. When they think no one else is watching, this is their chance to molest the baby or even physically abuse the baby.

Everyone can't tolerate crying. A screaming baby tends to make some people very angry. If they can't stop the baby from crying, they beat them or leave them in a separate room.

When I become a mother, I will do whatever is necessary so that I can stay home with my baby for two years. I don't want some man molesting my child. And not only do men molest children. There are women who have sick minds. They will also molest a baby.

Did you know that a woman can be molested at an early age and not remember it ever took place until she is an adult? I know of a woman who was molested at the age of four. For ten years, she had nightmares about her uncle molesting her. She thought it was a bad dream. Then one day while watching a talk show, she heard a psychiatrist discussing sexual crimes.

The psychiatrist explained how the mind has the ability to hide unwanted memories. A person can be molested and totally block the incident from their mind. The only problem with this is that the mind has a way of resurfacing emotions.

What happened to the lady shocked me. She listened to the talk show then visited a psychologist. A psychologist is similar to a psychiatrist. The only difference between the two is that the psychiatrist can write prescriptions, and the psychologist can't write prescriptions.

During her visit with the psychologist, she was hypnotized. The psychologist asked her to recall being four-years-old, which she did. All of a sudden, she was crying hysterically. She went back to a room of her youth. There in the room her uncle sat her on a table. He removed her panties, pulled her dress around her waist, and spread her legs wide.

At the tender age of four, she knew what he was doing to her was wrong. She sucked on her bottom lip and mumbled to him. "I want my mama. When is my mama coming home?" With a disgusting grin on his face, he responded, "She will be home in an hour." Tears bubbled in her eyes as he stuck his head in her private area. He continued by using his fingers and other objects to hurt the frightened four-year-old.

The psychologist helped the woman to confront a piece of the past, which she had forgotten. Coming to grips with the molestation helped her to understand why she always hated her uncle although everyone in her family loves him dearly.

Someday, I am going to own a daycare center. I can make it happen. I have to take some business courses to teach me how to get the proper licenses and business loans.

I remove my robe and undress. I step under a cold shower. Cold showers give me energy. I shower then towel dry. I put in my contact lenses then brush my teeth. I will get dressed then wake Patrick.

I return to the bedroom to get my bra and underwear. Patrick is wide awake. He has his arms behind his neck. He smiles at me as I enter the bedroom.

"I can't believe it. You are awake," I say.

"I wanted us to talk before you leave."

"Surprise, surprise. What do you want to talk about?"

"About the bills."

"What about them?" I grunt.

"You are spending to much money on junk."

"Excuse me. I am not the one running all over town spending money on hotel rooms."

"Neither am I," he says with a frowned face.

"We both know the truth. Don't we? Let's not get complicated."

"Shanna, you have no proof. All you do is accuse me of cheating."

"Patrick, I have an exam this morning. I am not going to get upset. I will talk to you this evening."

"Whenever I mention bills, you never want to talk."

I begin to ignore Patrick. I really do not want to discuss bills before I go to class. He pays to wine and dine other women. Why can't he help me with my bills? He can talk until he is blue in the face. I am not listening. I go into the closet, and grab a pair of jeans with a t-shirt. I walk into the living room to get dressed.

I get dressed and leave. Patrick is taking a shower. He will realize I am gone when he gets out of the shower.

Chapter Five

Class should be ending in five minutes. The professor gave the class two hours and thirty minutes to take the exam. In my case, he could have given us thirty minutes. My answers will still be the same. I have sat here the entire time pretending to know the material. I am frustrated. If it were not for my pride, I would turn in my exam and accept an "F". Instead, I will hang around just in case my subconscious mind kicks in.

Instead of going to bed last night after finishing my paper, I should have studied for this exam. My notes are very thorough. I could have earned a "C" by studying my notes. I should have studied for an hour. I did not bother to review my notes before coming to class. I assumed I knew the material.

Some students have finished their exam, turned it in, and left. I, on the other hand, will wait until the last minute to turn in my exam. Maybe the professor will take this into consideration while scoring my paper. At least I appear to be in deep thought.

I think professors pay attention to students who turn their exams in early. The professor probably thinks that student rushed through the exam without analyzing the questions. I truly wonder if professors grade the exams turned in first harder than the other exams turned in after class ends.

I am taking an exam in Humanities Class. This is the hardest exam he has given so far. My mind is not focused on the questions. I keep hearing music in my head. It is blocking my ability to concentrate. This does not happen to me very often. I was listening to the radio on my way here to the campus. I would have turned the radio off if I had known it was going to affect me this way.

The song I am hearing in my head is a new release by an artist who was discovered while singing on television. He entered a singing contest and won. It is surprising a producer did not discover him before now. I am going to buy his CD when I get some spare money.

The desks in this classroom were created for skinny people. My arms are crammed and my legs are aching. These desks do not have enough space for me to move around without falling on the floor. Imagine sitting a six-year-old in a baby stroller. The feet and legs will drag on the floor, and the arms will hang over the sides of the stroller. It is almost impossible to fit a six-year-old child in a stroller unless the child is willing to be uncomfortable. And I have seen this happen in the mall. A mother may want to walk around the mall searching for bargains, but her child wants to go home. The mother will carry the baby in her arms, and let the six-year-old ride in the stroller.

I move my neck around in a circle. The muscles in my neck crack as I move from side to side then back and forth. I am tense. I need a massage.

This particular professor grades very hard. He marks the entire answer wrong if half of it is wrong. Why doesn't he give partial credit for attempting to answer the question? He smiles whenever the students ask for extra credit or a review sheet. He always says, "You are college students not high school students. I expect you to think on a college level."

Truthfully, he is not a good professor. He comes into the class, puts his briefcase on the table, and starts writing on the board. He does not greet the class or give the late arrivers a chance to get settled. And he always arrives on time. Ten minutes after class is scheduled to begin, he has enough information on the board to fill the front and backside of two sheets of lined paper.

There is a medium-size board in front of the classroom. He writes the information on the board, discusses it briefly, and then erases it to write more information. If a student asks him to slow down or leave the information on the board, he smiles and remarks, "Oh, I wish we could. There just isn't enough time in the semester to move like turtles. Remember, everything written on the board is covered in your textbook. If you do not copy what's on the board, read the assigned chapters."

His teaching method is horrible! He gives way to many questions and examples on the board. Some of his notes come from other reference material not found in our textbook. Does he really expect us to find those other books? If he was planning to refer to other resources, he should have included these resources on the Course Syllabus along with the textbook.

He does give homework assignments. I spend two or three days on each homework problem and have not received a perfect paper yet. When the exams come, he never uses the exact questions taken from the homework assignments. Instead, he scrambles the questions on the exam like an egg. His exams remind me of Easter. He always manages to throw in an essay question, which was hidden in the textbook. His objective is to make us sweat. It's like searching for Easter eggs in a cow pasture.

His exams are a maze. My patience is to thin for this pre-school trivia. He should be teaching Kindergarten students not college students. I would not recommend him to any student.

I think he loves to see his students squirm. He walks around the class during the exams watching the students. His facial expression is evil and sinister. He has no mercy. I am trying to do my best in this class without any assistance from him.

It is raining. The rain is pounding against the windows. The sky is blue-gray and gloomy. Lightning flashes across the sky. The thunder is enough to send my hands into a shiver. I hate thunder. I am already a nervous wreck.

This class meets twice a week on Tuesday and Friday morning at eight o'clock a.m. in Room 1333. Originally, the class was scheduled to meet on Tuesday and Thursday, but the professor changed the days because of a conflict with his schedule. This is a fairly large class. There has to be thirty or more students in here.

I arrived here this morning at seven thirty-five a.m. I passed the time by drinking a cup of vanilla flavored coffee. I usually drink hot chocolate with imitation marshmallows. I get it from the grocery store. I drank the last packet yesterday. I have to go grocery shopping soon to refill my cabinets.

I wanted something to eat before coming to class, but I did not want to eat a big breakfast before taking my exam. Eating a heavy breakfast makes me sleepy and restless. Eating any heavy meal makes me sluggish regardless of the time of day. I do eat heavy meals on the weekend because I get a chance to lounge around the apartment.

I drank my vanilla flavored coffee inside the classroom. I also did some meditation. Everybody has their own special way of meditating. Some people meditate by praying. Some people meditate by doing yoga. Some people meditate by sitting in a quiet place and focusing on positive things. There is no correct way to meditate. The individual does what suits them best.

There were some students sitting in the back of the class studying together. Studying with a partner helps reinforce what you already know. I envy them. They are friends.

I woke up this morning thinking about the conversation Desiree and I had last night. She is always on my mind even when I refuse to acknowledge her presence in my thoughts. After our conversation, I could not study. I was fortunate enough to finish my research paper. I will hand in my research paper with my exam.

I went to bed tired last night. I had planned to type my Bibliography Page then do the Review Questions in the back of the chapter. I also had plans to study my notes, but I was to tired to think about Humanities.

My boyfriend was asleep when I got into bed last night. I did not bother to wake him. The mere sight of him turns my stomach sometimes. And I did elbow him in the back. The man only wiggled. He did not stop snoring. Maybe I did not elbow him hard enough.

Since December, he has tried to treat me with respect. It is not working for me. I am sick of the same lies and excuses from him. There have been times when he has done me wrong, and I accepted his lame apology. I will not be accepting anymore of his apologizes. I want to be free of him. He has no other choice but to shape-up or ship-out.

He has done his share of cheating. I have argued with women about him. I almost went to blows with a woman who pulled a knife on me for him. He swore she was stalking him. I knew he was lying. Why would a total stranger stalk a man she does not know? He is not famous. He is not the best looking man in town. I called the police. She was arrested.

The State Attorney's Office sent me some papers

in the mail. They wanted to charge her with a felony. They wanted me to pursue the case by testifying against her in court. I did not bother. If they wanted to send her to prison, they had to do it on their own. I am a woman who understands what it is like to be hurt and used by a man. There is nothing worse than being in-love with a man who sleeps with you and then decides he does not want you. I know how bad it hurts. She was a wounded lover.

I knew Patrick was lying to me about this woman. She was not an unattractive woman. I was able to learn more about her by reading some of the court records. She had her own home and car. She had a job. She had no reason to stalk him unless he was actually dating her.

A woman can accept a man leaving her rather than staying with her and cheating. Deceit causes an awful feeling in the heart. Having a man tell you he loves you is intoxicating. You get hooked on his sweet words.

I knew my boyfriend was cheating before the incident with this woman and her getting arrested. I felt it in my heart. Something was wrong. His pattern changed. He was lying about his whereabouts. He was dressing differently. His mannerism in the bedroom blew me away. In the past, he was boring in the bedroom and afraid to try new things. Then all of a sudden he became more aggressive.

The day I met this other woman caught me off guard. I had been working all day. I was exhausted when I got home. She was parked in front of my apartment waiting to speak with me. I should have been more open-minded with her instead of going into defense mode.

Everything she said about Patrick was true. She described a scar on his leg. She told me about trips they had taken together. He took her to the same places he took me. The most startling thing she described about him was how he made love to her. He told her, "Can't you tell how much I love you by the way I make-love to you?"

My eyes widened after she spoke those words. I knew she was telling the truth. He tells me the same thing. Her voice was sincere.

Something within me hated her for being intimate with my man. From that moment on, I wanted to do damage to her. She slept with my man. This is a no-no.

I was ready to slap her. There she was on my territory telling me she was dating my man. I felt threatened. My suspicions were confirmed.

"Can we talk?" she asked me.

"We have nothing to talk about. I don't discuss my man with other women," I told her.

"He is my man and your man. I just want to stop all of the lies. He can be with you, or he can be with me. He needs to tell me the truth," she shouted.

"Obviously, he already told you the truth. Why else would you be here?"

"I came here to speak with you and him. I can't keep living like this." The hurt in her voice was very clear.

"Living like what? Sleeping with another woman's man." These words quickly left my mouth.

"Like I said, he is your man and my man. He is not married. He can date any woman he pleases. The only thing I want from him is the truth. It is to dangerous to have a man who sleeps with multiple women. No man is worth my life. AIDS is serious."

"You're stupid and dumb. Don't come here ever again, or I will call the police," I told her.

"Both of us are stupid and dumb. He is playing both of us."

I did not want to hear anything else she had to say. Her mentioning AIDS reminded me of Desiree. I have a sister living with the virus that causes AIDS. My sister is infected. I was not going to let some woman who I did not know give me a lecture on AIDS.

I could have overreacted, but I tried to remain calm. I called her some nasty names. She called me some nasty names. I threw my purse in the street and told her "Come on. What are you going to do?"

"I didn't come here to fight. I came here to talk."

"I have nothing else to say to you." I was ready for war.

"Now I see why he came to me. What man in his right mind would stay with you?" she asked.

"I know what man would stay with me, the man who will be here by six p.m. He is the man you came here for."

"I have tried to be nice."

"Well, try somewhere else." I threw my hand up.

She came on the wrong day. I was not prepared to deal with her. Life was already kicking my butt. My boyfriend was the least of my worries. I was mainly upset because she mentioned AIDS. She could have called him every name in the book, and I would not have responded.

"I have nothing else to say. Goodbye," I said.

"Don't walk away from me."

"Hold on. Stop the press. I said goodbye," I told her in a louder tone.

She was still talking when I retrieved my purse. I put my purse on my shoulder and closed my car door. I was determined to escape the situation before it got to heated. She was determined to make me listen to her.

As I attempted to walk pass her, she pulled a knife from her pocket. My big mouth was in trouble. My mother always warned me about talking too much. I stood motionless. She was ready to cut my throat.

"Now what? You had so much to say. Keep talking," she told me.

"I am not afraid of a knife. Go ahead cut me!"

I was afraid. I could not let her know I was afraid. Fear is a sign of weakness. I had to make her think I was ready to protect myself. I thought about grabbing for my Mace. It was inside of my closed purse.

She stuck the knife to my neck. I could feel the sharp edge sticking me. I stared her in the eyes. I was debating whether or not I should move. I stood there. She was so close to me; I could smell her breath.

"I should stab you. You have a big mouth. You talk too much. I guess you have met your match. Don't say a word. I don't have a problem with you. I have a problem with Patrick. The next time I come here, it won't be to talk. Give him a message for me. I am not playing anymore."

She stepped back. She never put the knife away. She knew I was going to attack her. She held the knife in the air until she was inside her car. I watched as she reversed from the parking space and drove away. I memorized her tag number.

There is nothing worse than two women fighting over a man. The man lies to both of them. He throws his rocks and hides his hand. He convinces both women she is number one. All along, he is sleeping with both of them. He tells both of them the same lies. The stupid women believe him.

Some men get pleasure from having women fight over them. They think it makes them macho to have two women degrading each other. A real man does not handle his business like a schoolboy. A real man would be embarrassed to have two women fighting over him in public. A real man can handle his business without getting caught.

There are so many men in the world who claim to be real men. They want to be referred to as a man, but they act like boys. Being born with a penis does not qualify a male to be a man. Behavior determines what qualifies a male to be called a man. Being responsible separates the men from the boys.

Many women have killed because of a man. When you play with somebody's emotions, you never know how he or she will react. In the heat of the moment, a person is capable of doing anything.

Patrick better dot his I's and cross his T's with

me. I am not going to deal with anymore cheating from him. The very next time another woman confronts me he has to go.

While worrying about my sister, I have no intentions of taking any junk from him. I do not care anymore. One thing for sure, he will not create any more stress for me. I have enough to deal with.

Last night, I wanted to wake him, and tell him to leave. I was tired of his snoring like a pig. He says he snores whenever he has a hard day. I do not know why his days are hard because he usually keeps his work a secret. He does not discuss many details about his job. Whenever I get on his case, he will only discuss minor details with me. Other than that, he is a liar.

He claims to be a workaholic. There is no way a man can work thirteen hours a day, six days a week and not have anything to show for it. He is behind on his bills and my bills. He knows I expect him to help me financially. He complains about paying my bills. I ignore him. The day he stops paying my bills is the day he can no longer live under my roof.

There have been occasions when I have

discovered receipts for hotel rooms. I have found plane tickets for him and other women in his wallet. When I confront him, he accuses me of spying on him. He tells me not to go in his wallet. He says I do not trust him enough, which is what all men say when they get caught cheating.

I am not going to compromise about his cheating. There are no more words to be said. He has heard all of my arguing and screaming already. I have argued with him until I am speechless. Actions speak louder than words. Actions will prove my point to him. I know he will start cheating again. Only this time, I will pack his clothes in a garbage bag, and sit them on the porch!

I kind of figure he is still cheating with an ex-girlfriend. I do not have any proof. I am basing my suspicions on mere speculation. He acts really weird whenever I mention her name. He gets angry if I question why he spends money on her kids. He is not their father. Darkness can not hide in the light. When the truth comes to the light, he better pray I am having a good day. The mood I have been in lately will cause me to do bodily harm to him. He knows what I am going through with my sister, and there is no reason for him to add any unnecessary pressure to my life.

If Patrick is cheating again, it is because I refuse to have sex with him. The man has been a dog to me. He has allowed women to come to my home. He has called women from my home. I have even driven by women houses late at night searching for him. Women have confronted him in my presence and told me he had oral sex with them.

I will never forget the first time I went searching for him. I found an address in his jacket. I knew it belonged to a woman. He tried to hide it from me.

He claimed to be leaving town to visit his family in New York. I think it was almost Christmas. His aunt supposedly died. I asked him what his aunt's name was. He hesitated.

He told me, "My aunt died. I am going to fly to New York to be with my family."

"What aunt? You never told me about an aunt living in New York."

"I did tell you my father's family lives in New York."

"You have gotten me confused with another woman. You have never mentioned any family members in New York."

"It is not my fault you don't listen to me."

"I listen very well. I do not want to argue with you. When are you leaving?" I asked him.

"Tonight"

"Tonight. No problem. Have fun," I told him.

I knew he was lying. I wanted him to think I believed him. I wanted him to think I was satisfied with his lie.

He took his suitcase to work with him. I refused to help him pack. He really did try to cover his tracks. I gave him a quick kiss before he left.

I spent the whole day watching television. I did not go to work. I was too anxious. I sat in my apartment reading magazines and sleeping.

Somewhere around midnight, I got dressed. I had already taken an address from his jacket. I hid it in the closet inside a pair of my shoes. I knew he would never discover it in my shoes.

I was ready to find him. I got the address from the closet, put my driver's license in my pocket, and locked my apartment's door.

The wind was blowing. The dark night frightened me. The streetlights shined dimly on the sidewalk. I walked over to my car. I had trouble opening the car's door because of the darkness. I was also nervous. A woman should not go anywhere alone at midnight. Rapists, perverts, and freaks come out at night.

I locked my car doors once I was inside. I used the windshield wipers to clear the fog from my windshield. The weather was chilly. I kept my body warm with the heater.

It was not difficult to find the address. I found it in less than thirty-minutes. The house was not far from my apartment. I was familiar with the area. The house was located in a new residential area constructed three years ago.

As I reached the corner, I slowed down and turned my lights off. I did not want him to see me. The woman's house was the fifth house on the right side. The house was big with an iron gate around it. The iron gate was tall and thick. I had to stop in front of the house because I could not see beyond the iron gate.

Guess whose car I saw? Patrick was there. I kept driving. I have never told a soul about this.

He is not my husband. We do not have any children

together. He has not given me an engagement ring. There is no wedding date. There is nothing holding us together. I am not even sure I love him. He has hurt me too much.

I am not willing to die for his love. It has gotten so bad between us. I do not trust him. He has agreed to wear a condom while having sex with me. Still, I say no. What if the condom breaks? I would get HIV. I am not playing Russian Roulette. Let him go ahead and sneak around. As long as I have my suspicions, he cannot touch me.

My sister's battle with HIV has opened my eyes. In the past, I was willing to do anything for love. I am wiser now. My life is more valuable to me. I have something to live for, my sister's children. I will not die for my boyfriend. Who's to say my boyfriend will be around in two or three years? Relationships come and go. He could ruin my life and then leave me. It happens everyday.

Relationships require dedication and commitment. Most couples know little about either, which is why more than half of the population gets divorced. Love is a foreign creature to most people.

The man who infected my sister with the HIV

virus had women by the busload. He had the money to lavish them with expensive gifts. He was also street smart. I can only imagine how many women he infected.

He was not man enough to tell my sister he infected her with HIV. Instead he ran to the health department and gave them a list of the women names he had been with during the past two years. My sister's name was on the list.

The health department called Desiree to inform her of the bad news. They gave her the option to get tested at the health department, or she could go to her primary physician. My sister chose to see her own physician to be more discrete. She did not want her business to fall into the wrong hands. All of Louisville goes to the health department when they do not have health insurance. Another bad thing about going to the health department is the unprofessional behavior of the people who work there. They probably knew my sister and would spread her business.

Desiree's doctor gave her the test. The doctor's office called her when the test results returned. They asked her to come in the office to see the doctor.

She went. The doctor sat her down in his office. He told her she is HIV positive. He explained how she can live, and be happy with proper treatment. The doctor also gave my sister a copy of her test results.

Desiree did not give me the complete details about what actually went on after she got the positive test results. I believe the initial shock of it all was enough to deal with.

One day, I will have no other choice but accept the fact my only sister has HIV. Until I do become more accepting, I will continue to be in this predicament. I am almost non-functional. My life has changed. My peace comes from being by myself, which is why I had to leave my job.

My job was there when I got there, and it will continue to be there. They can replace me. I do not care. They can fire me. I do not care. Life goes on. It has to go on. To be frank, I have no plans on returning. I told them I will be back. I lied. I did not want to leave on bad terms with my boss.

If or when my sister dies, I will do my best to regroup and raise her children. I will find a better job with benefits and more money.

Desiree's doctor told her she could live for

many years with proper medication and diet. This may all be true, but I see a long, black hearse in my head. All I keep thinking about is death. I see this long, black hearse rolling down the street. I picture my family driving away from a church after my sister's funeral. We are on our way to the cemetery. I see rain falling as I sit near my mother in the hearse. My eyes focus on the window so as not to look directly at my mother.

This is the worst daydream I have been getting since my sister told me she has HIV.

This entire ordeal is a nightmare for me. My sister has to stay alive. I will lose my mind if she dies. Fate is so unfair. I know Desiree has to pay for her sins, yet I am unable to deal with her sentence. She has been sentenced to death.

Life has been way to hard for Desiree already. I am tired of heartache. They say God won't put more on you than you can bear. I have to disagree. My sister's condition is killing me inside. They say God always gives a way out. What is Desiree's way out?

Well, the five minutes is up. The professor is calling for the exam. I open my purse to put my pencil inside. I am glad this is over.

Chapter Six

The exam is over, and I am heading to the parking lot. I do not have another class today. The professor smiled at me as I turned in my exam along with my research paper. I returned his smile. Smiling at the professor is a vital ingredient in my recipe. His smiling at me let's me know my recipe is working.

Louisville is a gorgeous city. In the Fall, the trees blossom with beautiful flowers. In the Winter, we get enough snow to make a snowman. In the Spring, the squirrels race down the oak trees. In the Summer, the sun's rays send the neighborhood kids to the swimming pool.

I have always lived in Louisville, Kentucky. I did travel to North Carolina once while I was in high school. I went with the school's band. We performed in a band competition.

Traveling is not important to me. I am easy to please. I am not interested in big lights or Hollywood. Just give me some watermelon when it is hot and some biscuits in the morning, and I am satisfied.

I attend the University of Louisville. The campus is huge compared to the local community college. I suspect there are universities in the United States much larger than U of L. Living in a small town does not require us to have a campus as enormous as Harvard University.

Most people have never heard of Louisville. Kentucky is not a popular state. It is a perfect state for families to settle down, and raise their children. Our crime rate is extremely low. We have our share of trouble as all states do. Indeed, it is safer to live in a small town rather than the big city.

I drive a brown Toyota Corolla. My car is my baby. I saved my money for years to purchase this car. Buying a car is my first big investment. There is nothing like being responsible. I sacrificed going to the movies, shopping, and splurging on junk to save money to buy my car.

As I walk across the campus heading to the parking lot, I see students everywhere. Some students are leaving the campus. Other students are rushing to class. I am lucky to be leaving.

I parked my car in the last row. I do not mind parking my car in the last row because the parking spaces are so tight here on campus. I get so mad when I come from class and find a car parked close to my car. I have noticed something about students who have old cars. They park very close to other cars and put dents in them. To avoid going through the hassle of paying to get dents removed from my car, I'd rather walk the extra distance.

Students do not want to walk a long distance when they come to class. They try to find the closest parking space to the campus. I like to walk. Walking keeps the heart healthy.

Before crossing the street, I pause at the Stop sign. Cars are supposed to stop at student crossing. I have seen cars drive right through student crossing and not bother stopping for the students. Maybe they do not understand the purpose of student crossing. Maybe they do not see the white lines painted on the road. There have not been any hit and runs on this campus. There is a first time for everything. I prefer the first time not begin with me.

I walk ahead looking for my car. My car is not in sight. I am near the second row of the parking lot. I have three more rows to go before reaching the last row, which is where I parked my car.

The street is covered with small puddles of water. I thought it would still be raining. Thank the heavens it is not raining anymore. My umbrella is in the trunk of my car.

I am not wearing a fancy outfit. I don't mind getting wet. I had to wear this outfit. I was too lazy this morning to iron. Besides, I wanted to get away from Patrick. His conversation this morning would have upset me if I entertained him. A woman has to know how to deal with stress and opposition. Every problem that comes along is not meant to stay.

I walk ahead in search of my car. The school security guard passes me on a golf cart. He is patrolling the parking lot. We do not have a high crime rate on this campus. The university should invest in a minivan to transport students across the campus. This is a better way to spend university funds. The security guard is getting paid to chill-out. All he does is ride around flirting with the ladies.

There it is, my Toyota Corolla. I am relieved. My legs are beginning to throb.

I continue to walk across the parking lot until I reach my car. Once I get to my car, I open the trunk, throw my book bag inside, and close it. With my purse in hand, I walk around to the driver's side of the car to open the door. The windows are electric. My passengers can operate their window by pressing a button on their door, or I can control all of the windows in the car.

I reach over the steering wheel, and place the key in the ignition. I roll down the car windows to release the heat from inside of the car. The heat is gone in seconds. I slide into the driver's seat, and roll the windows back up then turn on the air conditioner.

I sit here in my car with the air conditioner blowing and my music blasting. I breathe in through my nose and release the air through my mouth. I need this time to regroup. My life is going downhill. Life is kicking my butt. There is nothing I can do to prevent what is happening around me. I believe in God, but lately I am too angry to pray or trust in Him.

I feel like running. I will more than likely go to the track this evening. I am going to run until I pass out or fall down, whichever comes first. I can deal with both right about now.

The clock inside my car reads ten-fifty a.m. I shake my head from side-to-side, and place the car in reverse. I reverse from the parking space. I look in both directions while reversing my car.

I leave the school's parking lot and then get on Hemingway Road heading to my mother's house. My mother's house is a place of refuge for me. I can always go to her knowing she will make me feel better. My mother has a way of making me hold my head up when I am at my lowest point.

My mother and I have not always been this close. It took many trials to bring us where we are today, but I thank God for her.

A mother knows when her child is hurting

inside. If no one else in the world cares, a mother will do whatever she can to help her child.

My mother's house is not far from the university. I can get to her house in twenty minutes by speeding. All things considered, I cannot afford a speeding ticket, so I had better adhere to the speed limit – thirty m.p.h.

Traffic is not heavy. White collar workers usually begin working by nine a.m. School age kids are in school by eight a.m. The school buses won't be on the road again until one p.m. This frees traffic for drivers like me.

My mother lives on Davinia Road. The road was named after a six-year-old girl who was killed by a motorcyclist. A young man was driving a motorcycle with his girlfriend on the back. He was speeding down the road and lost control of his motorcycle. He could not prevent hitting the six-year-old girl. I was told he was placed on probation for ten years and ordered to do community service. I do not know what happened to his girlfriend. I think her leg was broken along with some scratches on the forehead.

I continue driving to my mother's house, and

listen to my radio. I see the same sites such as Mr. Brown's Hardware Store, Lucie's Bar and Grill, Piper Grocery, and so forth. I have seen these landmarks all of my life.

The closer I get to my mother's house the more satisfaction I feel. She is the only person alive who loves me unconditionally. She loves me with all of my faults. She gets on my case every now and then, but what mother won't chastise their child?

I begin to turn onto Davinia Road. My heart skips a beat. My mother is near. I sound like a big baby. It comes natural. Besides, in my mother's eyes, I will always be her baby no matter how old I get.

I drive for a few more minutes then turn into the yard, a sight for sore eyes. I park my car on the grass in front of her house. My mother's grass is not soft. There are spaces in the yard with absolutely no grass. She does not do anything special to keep the grass green. Willie cuts the grass whenever it grows extremely high. Willie owns a landscaping company. His business is small. He only has two employees, himself and his brother.

The vertical blinds are drawn closed in the living room. What is my mother doing in there?

Is she still asleep? Knowing her, she is in the bedroom watching television. It appears that she is not home, but I see her car. I know she is here. She wants people to think she is not at home.

This past year has not been easy for her. She keeps her house dark. Darkness is a sign of depression. I know my mother is depressed because she only started ignoring her friends after my sister told her about being HIV positive. My mother is ashamed to let her friends know the truth.

My mother always placed her daughters on a pedestal. Her friends would know we are not perfect if my mother told them my sister has HIV. Quite frankly, I do not know why she is concerned about what people think. It is none of their business anyway.

My mother used to work on her rose bushes in the yard when the season was right, or she would grow a vegetable garden. After my sister got sick, she lost interest in both hobbies.

I get out of my car, and close the door behind me making sure to lock it. My car keys are swinging in my hand as I walk in the direction of the house. I have a key to my mother's house. My mother gave me a key after my father moved into his own apartment. Even though I have my own apartment, this will always be my home.

I open the door and walk inside. It smells like mothballs in here. This house needs some fresh air. I will open the windows before I leave.

I do not see my mother. I think she is in her bedroom. I can hear the television blaring. I throw my car keys on the sofa, and walk down the hallway to find her.

In the bedroom door, I stand almost nauseous gazing in her direction. My voice squeaks. I can sense she is upset. I know when my mother has been crying. Her eyes get dark red with black circles underneath. Her nose becomes a funny shade of red.

I stand here waiting for her to acknowledge me. She looks at me then forces herself to speak.

"Shanna, are you finished with school so early? I thought your classes go until three o'clock."

"It depends on the day. I could have gone to the lab to do some studying, but I am not in the mood. My head hurts."

"Well, do what you can. Don't worry about the rest."

"I know, Mama."

My mother turns her head to focus on a T.V. Dinner. She has been trying to lose some weight. She is eating a weight loss meal. I am happy she is determined to get rid of those extra pounds. She has lost sixteen pounds already.

I am on a binge diet myself. My conflicts arise when stress hits me. I tend to eat food for comfort. I am an emotional eater. I do not eat big meals. I eat sweet candies and sweet cookies with way to many calories. I have gained three pounds this week alone. I was eating glazed donuts every second of the day. I got on the scale before leaving for class this morning. As I expected, I gained weight.

I really do want to lose weight, and keep it off. It is not easy. When I was much younger, I lost weight because I had more will power and control over my appetite. Also, I had fewer problems.

I want to lose weight, but my mind is bombarded with so many other things. I am having trouble accepting Desiree has HIV.

I write poetry. I started writing poetry in high school. My Language Arts Teacher was writing a book. He assigned his students to write poems to be included in his book. I wanted to see my name in a book, so I wrote a poem. He liked the poem. He included it on page ninety of his book. I was not paid any money for the poem.

I have a lot of poems in a box at home. I like to share my poetry because it expresses who I am. I want my poetry to influence other women. There are famous poets who forget where they come from. The only way to get a copy of their work is by buying their book, or paying them to do a seminar. I do not have a big ego. I think sharing my poetry for free is just as rewarding as selling poems for a fee. I am not famous, so there are no book clubs interested in my poems.

I entered a poem in the SaraMay Dandridge Poetry Contest last year. I did not win, but I was invited to attend the award ceremony. I wrote a long poem about being overweight and submitted it to the committee.

Cloud By Day, Fire By Night

I am addicted to food.

It has taken me a long time to face this fact.

I am a food addict always thinking about my next snack.

Every time I get upset, I run to the grocery store to get me a fix.

I eat chocolate donuts, chocolate cake, and chocolate candy.

I eat so much. It makes me sick.

I use to vomit to get rid of the food.

I had to stop. My dentist bill was more than I could afford.

I have eaten boxes of laxatives and foods high in fiber.

This did not make me lose weight. The numbers on the scale only went higher.

Weight loss centers use me as an example.

I have given them hundreds of dollars to make me thinner.

The weight loss only lasted for a couple of months.

I always go back to being fat.

I have a turkey chin, five rows on my side, a Santa Claus stomach, and cottage cheese thighs.

I am a prisoner of food. Food is "All Powerful".

A judge and a jury did not determine my life sentence.

Based on my eating habits, I am sentenced to death.

I know I am going to die if I do not put down the fork.

Food dictates to me. It controls my every thought.

It determines how I will live my life.

When I sneak and eat although I know it is wrong, I cry because
I am not strong enough to say "no".
I am unhappy in this ugly body.
Food is my worst enemy.
I wear warm jackets on hot summer days.
People laugh at me. They call me crazy.
I am not crazy. I am only guilty of being lazy.
I have tried every diet in the book.
None of them worked. Food has me hooked.
Every weight loss program in town has a file on me.
They have created special counseling just to deal with me.
Some of them call me at home. Some call me at work.
Some bother me so much I take my phone off the hook.
I know they mean well. They want me to succeed.
It is me with the problem. I constantly stay on my knees.
I am a food addict. And I have struggled all my
life to kick this habit.
Food has way too much control over me.
Every breath I breathe is based on what I eat.
When I black out in the middle of my bed, after eating too much,
I hear a voice saying,
"Shanna stop eating. Why are you doing this to yourself?"
I have tried to walk away.
The longest I have stayed clean is 36 weeks.

I leave the treatment center and drop by the store
to get something sweet.
I have an addiction I can't seem to kick.

Written by Shanna

I know this is a long poem, but I couldn't decide how to shorten the poem. I write with lots of emotions, and I want the reader to actually experience what I am describing. The only way a reader can experience an event is by reading a broad explanation. This is my opinion about writing; this is not a fact. Scholars would probably disagree with me.

You will not find this poem in any book. A famous poet did not write this poem. I wrote it. It is apart of my collection of poems. I dedicate this poem to all women who suffer from eating disorders. An eating disorder can be vomiting on the weekends. An eating disorder can be starving to fit into a dress. More than ninety-percent of the population has an eating disorder.

Losing weight is not found in an expensive gym or a starvation diet. Losing weight is not found in a bottle of diet pills. To lose weight, it requires spirituality, happiness, eating less, drinking water, and exercising. There is no other way to lose the weight.

"Did you speak with Desiree today?" my mother asks me.

"No, I have not called her. I spoke with her last night. She called me. I could tell she had been crying."

"What did she say?"

"She talked about not wanting to get out of bed. She does not want anyone to know she has HIV. She did talk to me about her kids. Desiree said she wants them to stay together. She does not want them to be separated if she dies. She thinks their paternal grandmother, Hannah, will try to get custody of them."

"How can she get custody of anybody? She has never done anything for those kids besides buy cheap gifts at Christmas time from the Dollar Store. I will have her in court so fast her head will spin. She will not have a chance to blink her eyes twice. I have proof of what I do for those kids. I really take care of them. There is no judge in America who would deny me custody." My mother's voice changes when I mention Hannah.

"Mama, I hate talking this way. Desiree can live with HIV for many years. When AIDS-related symptoms do invade her immune system, she can still live with proper treatment."

"God can work miracles. I know He will save my child. I spoke to Desiree not to long ago. I told her to get down on her knees, and ask God to heal her body."

My mother's words sadden me. I want to have faith in God. I want to believe He is going to heal Desiree. I know God healed people in the Bible. I see pastors on the religion channel healing people every night. I know it can be done. I only fear God's reason for allowing Desiree to get HIV is to teach her a lesson.

There are cases when God puts tragedy in our lives to make us a better person. For some of us, we would still be sneaking around doing wrong things if we hadn't gone through bad times. There are cases when God punishes us to test us. I wonder what God has in store for Desiree.

Will God allow Desiree to die because she made some mistakes in the past? God is merciful to us all. I am curious if His mercy is great enough to deliver a HIV victim from death. I am aware we will all die someday. I may go before Desiree. No man knows the day or hour of his own death unless he commits suicide.

I continue listening while my mother speaks. I have my own thoughts racing through my head. Her voice appears far away when certain thoughts cross my mind. How can God heal Desiree's body? She has HIV. I have read about children being born with the virus and then testing negative as they grew older. I have never read about an adult contracting the virus and being cured. There has not been a single incident where an adult has tested positive for the virus then tested negative. I think the only way this will happen is if somebody tampers with lab results making them unreliable or invalid.

My mother is having trouble facing the truth. She keeps trying to convince herself it is not HIV. She keeps on making a new excuse everyday. Someday, she will have no other choice but to face the truth.

Some people are prejudiced against AIDS victims. We have not told anyone outside of our immediate family about Desiree. This is confidential information. My friends do not need to know. Desiree is my blood sister. And blood is thicker than water. Desiree comes before any of my friends.

My mother is in denial. Why mothers carry their children burdens on their shoulders is beyond me. I always thought a child begins to carry their own burdens after they turn twelve-years-old. Mothers never seem to let go. A mother thinks she is responsible for her child at any age.

"You know Shanna, I think Desiree could be faking. I looked at her yesterday, and her stomach has gotten bigger. Maybe she is pregnant and to embarrassed to tell us. I cannot believe it is HIV. No mother in her right mind can say something she brought into this world has HIV."

"Mama, she is not pregnant. You know what it is."

"I told Desiree to get another test in six months. It is sure to be negative."

"Mama, come on. You are making this more difficult for all of us."

My mother stops speaking and runs into the bathroom. I can hear her vomiting. She cannot hold any food in her stomach when the topic of AIDS is mentioned. She has been going to the doctor almost everyday. The doctor gave her some blood pressure pills. Her nerves are bad nowadays.

I stand here in her bedroom door with tears rolling down my cheeks. My lips tremble as I cry. Why HIV? This is the worst thing to ever happen in our family. Never before has any news touched us so deep. I mean this is ripping us to shreds. Little by little we are all dying.

I hear my mother flush the toilet, and turn on the water. I assume she is washing her face. When the water stops, my mother appears again and lies down on her bed. She is crying; I am crying. We are not offering each other any support. Sobbing noises and sounds from the television fill the room.

My mother is so pitiful. I wish I knew how to comfort her. Our family will eventually have to attend counseling. A trained professional, who knows about HIV and AIDS, could teach us how to cope with an infected family member.

I leave the bedroom door, and sit on the floor near the bottom of my mother's bed. I reach over to touch her feet with my trembling hands. Her body is warm. I pray she is not sick. I think she has a fever. She has a doctor's appointment scheduled for tomorrow morning. Her blood pressure is probably high. She has dark circles around her eyes. Her eyes are blood shot red. My mother is drifting away. Lately, her mind comes and goes.

Her appearance has gone down the drain. Her hair is damaged. She needs a perm and a trim. I have told her to go to the beauty salon before she loses all of her hair. She can even get her hair cut in a style. Any hairstyle is better than lying around here looking this way. Whenever I mention the beauty salon to her, she says, "I will go on the weekend."

"Shanna, I did everything a mother could do. I told you all about protection. Desiree cannot say she did not know. I begged her to leave that no-good man alone. A mother knows. God gives a mother instincts. When I saw him, something shot through me. I got a strange sensation in my chest near my heart. I knew he was trouble. Desiree has never listened to me."

"Mama, it is not your fault. We made our own

decisions in life. You did what any mother does. You set the example. We refused to follow your example. I do not blame you for anything that has happened in my life. You tried to protect us."

"That nasty bastard does not care what he has done to Desiree. He could have known he was infected when he slept with her. He is angry with all women," my mother tells me.

When my sister told me she has HIV, I immediately knew it was from Robert. He is a true dog. The lady from the health department had to be professional when she called my sister. She could not violate patient confidentiality. Desiree begged the lady to tell her the person's name who wrote the list. The lady told my sister, "You can call out some names. If you call the wrong name, I will say no. If you call the right name, I will remain silent. This is all I can do for you." When my sister said Robert, the lady remained silent.

In the beginning of this ordeal, I lost all sense of self-worth. I was planning to pay him a visit at his house, and burn it to the ground. I was not thinking. I forgot all about his kids and his mother who lives with him. I wanted sweet revenge.

Time has caused me to become more rational. I admit; I still have thoughts about seeking revenge. I want to see Robert suffer. Why didn't he come to my sister like a real man? Who knows how long he knew about his condition. For some odd reason, I think he infected my sister on purpose.

I do know one thing for sure. When my sister gets sick, he better hide. It will take everything within me to stay calm and not kill him. I am capable of doing such a thing if the right buttons are pushed. If my sister dies before I come to grips with this, I swear to God Robert will not live a week after we bury her in the grave.

I will go to the gun shop, and purchase a gun. I know I can get a gun with no problem. I do not have a criminal record. I have never been in trouble with the law. I have never been arrested. My record is clean.

I can have a gun in ten days or less. I can also buy a gun from a thug on the street corner. It will be cheaper. The gun does not have to be fancy as long as it shoots bullets.

I know exactly where Robert lives. I have been to his house with Desiree. I can find his house again.

He thinks he has the right to take a life. Then what goes around comes around. I will wait for him behind the big oak tree when it is dark. Forget about AIDS killing him. I will unload the gun in his head, and wait for the police to arrest me. Then his family will feel the same grief we will feel if my sister dies. All in all, both families will grieve due to a senseless act.

What will I gain from killing Robert? Nothing much because he will be dead. The most I will gain is the satisfaction that his mother and kids will feel the pain of losing a son and a father. People do not understand another man's pain unless they actually walk in his shoes. Likewise, the idea of an eye for an eye does not hurt.

I know the Lord says vengeance is mine, but what is the Lord going to do about my sister besides let her die? The ability to heal her is within His power. Has He healed her? No.

"Alex was beaten up last night," my mother tells me then changes the topic.

Alex is her brother. He has his own problems as well. He should try to get his life together. No one else can continue bailing him out of trouble.

He is a grown man. He better take a good look in the mirror, and decide what he wants to do with himself instead of draining the family emotionally with his weekly drama.

"Who did it?" I ask.

"He will not tell me. He says he does not know who did it. They caught him while he was going home from the club."

"Did they steal anything from him?"

"Not that I know of."

I think to myself. He is either telling a lie, or he crossed somebody. And they gave him a whipping. You cannot cross people these days and not suffer the consequences. People are crazy. They do not fear going to prison.

"Where is he now, Mama?"

"He is at home. He went to the Emergency Room. They stitched his forehead and sent him home."

"He will be alright. This is another warning for him."

"Emmanuel had a car accident earlier today. He is still in the Emergency Room. I told Brenda to call me when the doctor let's them know something about his condition," my mother tells me.

Emmanuel is my mother's oldest brother. Brenda is his wife. Emmanuel is nothing like Alex. He holds a sentimental place in my heart. He cares for me like a father unlike Alex who only cares about himself.

Emmanuel will do whatever he can to help anyone. I know he will be okay. A man ran the red light on Peach Street. He crashed into Emmanuel's car. Emmanuel then hit the car in front of him. "Emmanuel's car is totaled," my mother says. It could have been worse. At least he is not dead. He walked away with all of his limbs and his life.

The telephone rings as we continue our conversation. My mother reaches across her bed over to the nightstand. She answers the telephone on the third ring. I can tell it is a family member. It has to be my aunt because my mother's face begins to glow.

My aunt asks my mother to tell me hello. I am not going to hang around here much longer. I am satisfied knowing my mother is speaking with my aunt. My aunt is a very funny lady. She can make a person laugh when they are at their lowest.

I move away from my mother's bed as she talks to my aunt. I go into the kitchen to drink some water. I use a green cup and fill it to the very top with ice, cold water. After I drink the water, I place the cup into the sink and go into the living room to get my car keys. I yell to my mother in her bedroom.

"Mama, I will call you later."

"Okay, Shanna. Make sure you lock the door."

My mother does not bother to come into the living room. She is focused on her telephone conversation, which is fine with me. I do not want her to be lonely.

My mother and father are not living in the same house anymore. She told him to get his own apartment. They were always arguing and fighting. They both agreed living under a different roof is the only way to save their marriage. I disagree. A husband and wife should live in the same house.

I drop by to see my father occasionally whenever he is at home. He works a lot. He pays his bills, and helps my mother with the mortgage. He has always been so considerate and family oriented. He wants to move back in the house with my mother. She is not ready for him to come home.

I open the windows in the living room. The windows are already open in my mother's bedroom. I pull the string to open the vertical blinds. My mother will close the vertical blinds when she sees I have opened them. She prefers to stay in this pitch, dark house.

I unlock the front door and walk out. I close the door behind me. Then I lock the door. I will call my mother soon to check on her.

I walk down the sidewalk to my car. The sky is a weird shade of blue. The clouds are ivory white. The birds are in the sky. The only disorder is in my family.

Inside my car, I turn on the air conditioner. The radio comes on when the keys start the ignition. The air conditioner blows my air freshener hanging from the mirror making it wiggle in circles.

As I reverse my car, my heart pounds in my chest. I am lost in this big, gigantic world with no idea of how to establish a solid foundation.

My next stop will be the park. I will go to the park, and get on the swings. I like to swing with my legs high in the air and my head held backwards. What I would not do to go back in time when I was a little girl on the merry-go-round with pigtails.

Desiree and I went to the park when we were kids. We would take turns pushing each other in the swings. The ironic part is that we grew up going to the same park I am heading to at this very moment.

On Sundays, my mother and father would take both of us to the park. Sundays were family days for us. Monday through Saturday was another story.

Life was so much easier then. Our parents took care of everything. Our biggest worry was hurting ourselves while playing kickball in the street.

The park is no more than ten minutes away. I take my usual route. I pass the post office along the way.

As I turn down the street leading to the park, I stop my car in front of a brown house. I know the people who own this house. I have known them all of my life. They are Mr. and Mrs. Romeo. My sister loves Mrs. Romeo dearly. Mrs. Romeo gave my sister piano lessons.

I want to go inside and say hello to them. I better not. They will question me about Desiree. I would have to lie. I would never tell them she has HIV. I start my car again, and I drive away.

I reach the park to find several young men

sitting on a bench. They should be in school or working. They should not be here at this park in the middle of the day doing absolutely nothing.

I park my car in a space on the far side of the park near a big tree. The tree has lots of limbs. It provides shade for my car.

I roll my seat back to allow myself to get comfortable. Before thinking about what happened at my mother's house, I begin to cry.

"Please, please Lord. We need you so much."

I scream these words inside of my car. My windows are not down. No one can hear me. Even if they do hear me, they do not know me. Anything happening inside of my car is my business.

With every teardrop that falls, I let go of held in anger. Why is it raining in my life? My tears are like rain.

"Come rain," I say. "Pour down on this ragged body. Drown my fears. Wash away this day."

I might as well stay here at the park for a while. It is best I do not drive. I am capable of driving myself into a lake. I am hurting inside. Can anybody understand me? I feel like I am losing my sister. When it rains, it pours.

Chapter Seven

Oh, the years have gone by so fast. Not to long ago, my sister and I were children. And now she has children. To me, it seems most of the life span is spent as an adult. We get a few charity years as children. Then the table turns, and becoming an adult is not an option. I refer to childhood years as charity years because a parent or guardian has to supply their child with everything — clothes, food, and shelter. They give all of this for free, at no charge.

I come to the park many days when I want to

be alone. This park is not like other parks around town. There is a security guard on duty twenty-four hours a day. The Home Owner's Association ruled in favor of adding the cost for a security guard into the association fees. The security guard monitors the pool and the playground area. Children come to the park after school. It would not be a safe park for children if drug dealers were hanging around or predators were on the prow.

Around six o'clock p.m., elderly people come to the park to walk around the track. They are so energetic. They have formed a walking group. All of them meet at the park around the same time. They can beat me walking around the track. It is good to know they care about their health and weight. Not only is walking beneficial for their cardiovascular system, it gives them a chance to meet new people.

I visited a nursing home some years ago with a missionary group from my church. I had to quit the group. The nursing home environment was too sad for me. The elderly people were sitting around in wheelchairs sleeping, forced to sleep in urine-soiled beds, and asked not to bother the busy nurses on duty. The part, which got me, was an elderly woman screaming to the top of her lungs. She was screaming, "Somebody kill me. Kill me please. I don't want to live anymore. Just let me die."

Needless to say, I have not been back to the nursing home. I have a weak stomach. A nursing home should not smell like feces and urine. A nursing home should not be gloomy. Hiring an Activities Director should change the atmosphere in a nursing home. Being allowed to dance, do arts and crafts, and go on trips would keep the elderly vibrant and alive.

Elderly people are in nursing homes as a result of many different reasons. Their children may not be able to care for them. They are very ill. All of their family members have died. They need constant medical care, or they can't provide for themselves. It is a hard decision to place a parent in a nursing home. There is more guilt than anything else.

It is a big sacrifice. Children who work full-time jobs are not available to become informal caregivers for their parents. They have to work.

America has its' priorities backwards. We pay more money to watch an athlete run with a ball in his hand then we do for healthcare services for the elderly. Nursing homes would not be so bad if the government invested more money into maintaining these long-term care facilities.

Another burning issue neglected by the government is Medicare. Medicare offered to the elderly has many stipulations. A person has to be sixty-five years of age or older with few assets. Medicare offers two different plans: A and B. Plan A does not require a fee. Plan B requires the enrollee to pay a small fee. Medicare is a total injustice. It is one of the worst health insurance providers. The physicians, pharmacists, specialists, and hospitals who participate in the network care more about saving the provider money than they do about the elderly. Each year, it is reported 1 out of every 5 persons file complaints against Medicare.

The air conditioner in my car is blowing on full speed. I like it this way. If only I could blow all of my problems away at such a high speed, I wouldn't have to worry anymore.

What is the deal with scientists? Some of them claim to be geniuses while others believe they have the answer to everything? If they are so smart, why can't they find a cure for AIDS? How is it possible for scientists to clone animals and human beings, and not find a cure for the AIDS virus? Cloning has to be more complex.

Scientists in Australia have found a cure for Sickle Cell Anemia. This is a medical breakthrough. I read a journal article seven years ago about an Australian doctor who was in the process of giving a bone marrow transplant to a black child. The surgery was thought of as being dangerous, but the child was dying anyway.

The Australian doctor did perform the surgery. It was a success. The boy survived. American doctors have waited all these years to actually follow in the footsteps of this Australian doctor. Many lives could have been saved if only bone marrow transplants were given before it was to late.

Sickle Cell Anemia is a painful disease. I took a Speech Communication Course at the university. We were assigned to do a presentation. The presentation had to last for fifteen minutes. I chose to talk about Sickle Cell Anemia. I worked very hard preparing my slides and visual aids. I was so upset because none of the students had ever heard of Sickle Cell Anemia. The students were talking and laughing during my presentation. They were so rude to me.

What many people don't know is that Sickle Cell Anemia is a debilitating disease. A person who has Sickle Cell Anemia may not live to see their twentieth birthday. Sickle cells are not normal and round as in healthy persons. This happens because the cells are shaped like a sickle. Think of a sickle used to cut grass. It looks almost like a half moon.

Sickle shaped cells do not move freely in the bloodstream. These abnormal cells stick together in the veins preventing oxygen from flowing in the body. This is dangerous. A Sickle Cell Attack occurs if the cells do not untangle themselves.

During a Sickle Cell Attack, the person may need to be hospitalized. In severe cases, a blood transfusion is necessary. Sickle Cell Anemia patients suffer their entire life. They can never predict when an attack will occur. They miss a lot of days from work. If their boss does not understand the disease, usually they get fired from their job.

There is a difference between the Sickle Cell

Anemia and the Sickle Cell Trait. Sickle Cell Anemia is the disease. Sickle Cell Trait is the gene. If two people have the Sickle Cell Trait, and they have a child, the child may be born with Sickle Cell Anemia. If only one person has the Sickle Cell Trait, and their partner does not, their child will be born normal. If one person has Sickle Cell Anemia and their partner has the Sickle Cell Trait, their child will be born with Sickle Cell Anemia. I know this is hard to comprehend, but doctors advise people who have the disease or the trait to get their partners tested. The test is simple because Sickle Cell Anemia and the Sickle Cell Trait are genetic.

Persons with Sickle Cell Anemia look very young. They can be seventeen-years-old and look like they are twelve-years-old. Their bodies have discovered the fountain of youth.

Because people are so afraid of AIDS and HIV, they may misinterpret Sickle Cell Anemia symptoms as AIDS symptoms. Being paranoid makes you fearful of any illness. And fear paralyzes the mind.

I think AIDS is similar to the Black Plague. The AIDS virus will kill millions before a cure is found.

The next generation on Earth will read about how we struggled with AIDS just as we read about the Black Plague while sitting in our high school Social Studies Class.

There are many speculations about how the Black Plague got started. The Domino Effect has occurred in our day and age. There are many speculations about how AIDS got started. I really do dislike when a specific group of people is blamed for starting the virus. In the early seventies, rumor had it that gay men started the virus. Then people went on to suggest the virus was started in Africa by a certain species of monkey. Next, I heard gossip about Haitians starting the virus. All in all, we can blame whomever we chose for starting the virus. Point being, rumors, gossip, and mere speculation will never cure the virus. We should all be trying to find a cure instead of discriminating and crucifying someone for starting the virus.

While sitting here in my car, stupid thoughts cross my mind. They say it is best to cremate a body when a person dies from AIDS. Why should their bodies be cremated if their family wants them to have a regular burial?

I saw a drunk, older man at the corner store, sitting at the store's entrance, and letting the world have a piece of his mind. He was arguing with an invisible person. He would talk to customers going in the store if they would stop to listen. Me, being the kind-hearted person that I am, stopped to listen to him. I respect my elders.

He must have read my mind. Would you believe he started talking about AIDS? The man said, "We can't be burying those AIDS patients in the ground with other folk. Their body got a disease. That stuff like acid. When they put those bodies in the ground, the fluid from their body goes into the earth. We could all be drinking contaminated water or eating contaminated food. Before you know it, we all gone die from AIDS." His statement really disturbed me. How can body fluid get into the earth? A corpse is embalmed before it is put in the casket. I blamed his statement and ignorance on the alcohol. They do say a person exaggerates when they are drunk.

I am so fortunate I can be in a place where there is no noise. I can stay here all day crying, and not a soul would bother me.

I keep CDs in my car. My CDs have really old songs on them. I do not believe any of them are up-to-date. I can appreciate songs from the sixties, seventies, or the eighties. The music from those days has a message. The singers did not sing about junk. Many days when I listen to the radio I shake my head in disbelief. It is shameful how radio stations play songs with no meaning or message.

The young singers either sing to fast or sing about big cars, fancy clothes, or lots of money. And the veteran singers do whatever they can to compete with the younger singers.

Music has changed for the worse if you ask me. There were days when everybody listened to music because they could learn something such as how to be a better man, or how to appreciate family, or how to have a family reunion. I remember going to house parties in the neighborhood. At these house parties, everybody from miles around would come to sing, dance, eat, and have fun. The DJ played songs while crowds of people gathered in circles singing the lyrics. Children ran around playing hide-go-seek with soda cans in their hands. Parents didn't have to watch their every move in fear a child molester would grab them.

Times have changed. A house party is the last place I would be today. There is way too much violence from handguns and weapons. Let's not mention drugs and drive-by shootings.

Music is so trivial. It has a big influence on the mind. Have you noticed a person listens to music to suit the mood they are in? A person may listen to love songs when they are happily in-love. Kids may listen to rap music because it talks about defiance of authority. Aromatherapy is music, which imitates a calm sound like the beach or crickets. A tired person listens to aromatherapy music. It is a proven fact babies are smarter when their mother plays classical music for them while they are in the womb. A person with bad nerves wouldn't listen to Hip-Hop music.

AIDS Awareness Week is coming up soon. Mayor Spears asked a local rap group to create an AIDS Awareness rap for this year's activities. All of the radio stations are playing this rap song. The schools are playing this rap song during their AIDS Awareness assemblies. Even the grocery stores are playing this rap song. The local rap group has become famous in Louisville. Once again, music has the power to influence the mind.

All of the government owned businesses, the schools, the libraries, and the local health departments sponsor educational activities for the public. I attended the march for AIDS some years ago. I did not participate a second time. I was embarrassed when they sent a flyer to my home with the words *AIDS* across the top. I was afraid the mailman would see those words and automatically assume someone in the household had AIDS. I called the AIDS-Network and demanded they discontinue sending me any form of literature. They have to be careful. All of their information should be enclosed in a sealed envelope with no return address. If they do place their return address on the envelope, it should be in small letters.

When the flyer arrived at my house, I thought it was a vicious prank. It was from the AIDS-Network. I didn't give them permission to send me anything. My father saw the flyer before I did. He called me into the kitchen. He had a serious look on his face.

He said, "Shanna, do you need to tell us something?"

"Like what?" I asked.

"You know what I am talking about. Why are these AIDS flyers coming to my house?"

"That's nothing. I gave them my address when I walked in the AIDS marathon."

"You can't have that stuff coming to my home. Go get yourself a P.O. Box. Let them send it there. I won't tell you this again. And if you are sneaking around, whatever is in the dark will come to the light. You lie down with dogs, you will get fleas," my father said.

I sucked my teeth and walked in the living room. My mother was sitting on the sofa eavesdropping. She knew what our conversation was about. There was no such thing as a private conversation in our household unless it was between Desiree and me.

I think I will call the AIDS-Network to request some brochures to read. I never imagined I would want to become associated with them. Back then it was a choice. Today I am forced.

I can't stay here all day crying. My tears are wetting my t-shirt. The teardrops are turning the pink areas of the t-shirt to light orange. My entire t-shirt will soon be soaked. I despise having to go home to an empty apartment.

Chapter Eight

Eventually, I decide to leave the park, and go to my apartment. I roll my seat up, and lock it in place. I do not want it to slide while I am driving. I reach over to the radio, and put the CD on pause. I will drive home in silence.

I reverse from the parking space. I switch gears then drive forward. My car drives very smooth. I always keep the oil and filter changed regularly. I wash it myself once a week. I vacuum inside my car on Saturday. I like my car to be clean. A clean car represents how a person takes care of their home. A clean person would never drive around in a nasty car. A person who keeps their home filthy typically keeps their car filthy.

As I drive down the same street, which I took to get to the park, I see a young girl and a young boy walking down the sidewalk holding hands. I can only roll my eyes in disgust. This young girl should be in school or at home doing something productive. She should not be here with this young boy getting ready to do God knows what.

She does not realize in a few months this young boy will be a hidden face in the crowd. He will see her in school, and treat her as if he never knew her. If she is lucky, he will stay with her until after graduation from high school. This will only happen if she does not have sex with him.

Males learn early in life to fight for a challenge. Females who make them wait for sex are the winners. Females who give in early are the losers.

Think about it. After they have gotten sex, why should they stay? Men fear falling in-love, so if they do not love you, they will move on to the next challenge.

I know there are those who say I am bitter and angry. I do not think I am a hundred percent bitter and angry. Okay, I am angry but not bitter. My life experiences have made me the woman I am today. How can I talk about what I do not know about? In my life, the men have "sexed" me and left me. None of them stayed. They were not planning to spend the rest of their life with me. I wanted it to be forever. They wanted the moment.

Uncle Sam is looking for a few good men. Well, Uncle Sam will be looking until the cows come home because there is a shortage of good men. There are some good men left in the world, but they are hiding under a rock. The men who I have dated are not good men. It just so happens the man I am currently dating is not a good man. He is a liar, a dog, and a cheat.

I have stayed with him this long for stability. He pays the bills. He takes me on trips. He can be romantic. He prevents me from getting lonely at night. I accept him for these reasons.

I will not be with him forever. I did want to spend eternity with him before I discovered he was cheating with other women. I would be miserable marrying him knowing I will never be the only woman in his life. With him, there will always be somebody else.

I blamed myself for his behavior. I thought it was my fault. I wanted to be perfect for him. I did everything to keep him happy. I colored my hair. I bought a new wardrobe. I went on a diet. I cried for him. I begged him to treat me right. You name it; I did it to keep him satisfied.

I am turning down Oakland Road. I see a big, white house. It is sitting on a hill surrounded by a lot of land. There are some flowers near the porch. The porch has a big, white swinging chair in front of a glass window.

I will be at my apartment soon. I have a nosy neighbor. Her name is Cassandra. She is a nice lady, but she talks too much. Cassandra is a retired Correctional Officer. She spends her days sitting in a chair in front of her apartment. She watches the neighborhood. She sits in her chair the entire day. I have seen her reading the newspaper or a book. I think she is lonely.

Instead of sitting in her chair all day, she should go walking or jogging. Cassandra is not a spring chicken. She always wears tight shorts and scandals. Her thighs are huge. I do not have the legs of a model, but my legs are not that big. And I do not walk around in public with shorts revealing my butt. Cassandra is too old to be dressing so provocative.

I am not in the mood to talk with Cassandra. I will tell her I have a headache. This will free me of having to spend an hour shooting the breeze with her about what is happening in the news. Nothing exciting happens here in this town. Watching a late night movie on Channel 10 is more exciting than this town.

I press down on the gas pedal. I am doing forty-five m.p.h. This is enough to cause me to get a speeding ticket if a police officer is nearby. Since I do not see a police officer, I will take my chances. I want to be in my bed with the covers pulled over my head.

I continue to drive. This is the last traffic light I will have to adhere to before I get home. These traffic lights can be irritating. 10-9-8-7-6-5-4-3-2-1-0-0-0-0! Why is it taking this traffic light so long to turn green? I continue to count while waiting.

The traffic light finally turns green. I squeeze the steering wheel tight. I make a sharp left turn. My tires make a squeaking sound. I drive on. They are my tires. I can damage them if I please.

I see a beige-and-white apartment complex. I am here. Some of the apartments in this complex are beige with white trimming. The apartments in the back are ivory with black trimming.

I look in the direction of Cassandra's apartment to see if she is sitting in her chair. Thank you Jesus! She is not there. She must be ill. Maybe she is inside using the bathroom.

I drive ahead, and park my car in front of my apartment. Before exiting my car, I place the "club" on my steering wheel. I grab my purse. I walk rapidly to my front door. I do not want to see Cassandra. I am quite sure she is nearby. I try not to shake my car keys. The sound of car keys will bring her to the door. It is a shame I have to sneak into my own apartment.

I stick the key into the door. I do not mind sneaking today. Let Cassandra catch the next person who comes home. Let them listen to her talk about this boring town.

I smile while opening my apartment door. I enter my apartment. I close the door and lock it. I can smell the aroma candles. I love to have lots of candles in my apartment. My favorite candles are those with the aroma of sunflowers. I buy most of my candles from the Yankee Candle Company.

I burn my candles at night to prevent the apartment from being too dark. The candles make marvelous shadows on the walls. The shadows dance until the candles melt.

When I started dating Patrick, we took candles with us on picnics in the park. We even lit them in the bathroom while we showered.

We are not close anymore. I will never again consider using a candle with him in a romantic way. If I were to use a candle with him, it would be to pour the hot wax on his body to hear him scream for mercy. He deserves to hurt for all the pain he has caused me.

I want to have a man who I can sit down to the table with and talk. It does not matter what we talk about. I just want to be able to communicate with him. I want a man who I can relate to. I want a man to hug me. Late at night, when Patrick is somewhere with another woman, I get frustrated about my sister.

Patrick falls asleep when he is here. He forgets I

am in the apartment with him. He sleeps anywhere in the apartment. He sleeps on the couch. He will fall asleep on the floor in front of the television. He will then come to bed around three or four in the morning.

I go to bed late whenever I am studying. He will pretend to be sleeping when I get in bed. I can tell he does not want to be next to me at times.

If I go to bed before he does and he crawls into bed later, his body movement disturbs me. Sometimes, he will try to be intimate. I do not want him to do me any favors. He acts like touching me is a chore half of the time. I tell him to save it for the next woman. He is a thorn in my side.

Desiree is lucky. Her boyfriend is not going anywhere. He is not cheating on her. He wants to marry her. He is unique. I know I would not be as understanding as he is with Desiree. If Patrick ever came to me and told me he is HIV positive, I would beat him down to the ground.

Chapter Nine

I know there is so much more to be learned about AIDS and HIV. I am going to buy some books to educate myself. There has to be something I can do to improve Desiree's quality of life. I can educate Desiree's kids about what is happening to their mother. I can teach my mother about the virus. Somebody in the family should be educated enough to understand the virus.

I am not ready to attend any AIDS or HIV meetings. The people there might think I am infected. Someone who knows me might see me in the meetings. I don't want someone to see me attending a meeting and slander my name.

My apartment is comfortable. I have all the basic necessities in my apartment to help me survive. I may not have expensive furniture or a huge apartment, but I have shelter and a place to rest my head. This is all a middle class person can ask for. Patrick may or may not be here tonight. He has his own key. He can let himself in.

I take off my shoes at the door. I unzip my pants as I walk down the hallway to the bathroom. Inside the bathroom, I take off all my clothes, and throw them on the floor. I have to use the toilet before I go to bed. I am going to sleep early. I am not hungry. I just want to sleep this day away. Dealing with my burdens will be easier in the morning after a good night's sleep.

I wash my hands before removing my contact lenses. I grab the container for my contact lenses and the contact lens solution from the cabinet. I remove my contact lenses then rinse them with the solution before placing them into the container.

My doctor told me to remove my contact lenses before going to bed at night. My eyes get red and scratchy whenever I sleep in my contact lenses. I unknowingly rub my eyes in my sleep. This could cause a serious eye infection.

I am not going to shower tonight. I showered this morning before leaving for school. I also put on deodorant and body spray this morning. I can wait until tomorrow morning to shower. I am ready to go to sleep.

I walk into my bedroom. The sight of my bed gives me a cuddly feeling inside. I pull the sheets back, crawl underneath, pull them over my head, and fall asleep.

CHAPTER TEN

I can't believe I slept all night. My boyfriend did not come over. He did not call to say a word. My mother has not called. Desiree did not call.

I roll over to look at the clock. It is six forty-five a.m. It is not normal for me not to receive any calls during the night. This is odd. I reach down beside my bed to get the telephone. It is not on the hook. This explains it. I knocked the telephone off the hook when I was getting into bed. I should have heard the beeping sound or the operator's voice notifying me the telephone was not on the hook.

I was mentally exhausted when I got here yesterday. I could have heard the beeping sound and the operator's voice. I was so depressed and sad. I was not functioning properly.

I can relate to a person who says they were temporarily insane when they committed a crime. Insanity comes and goes like the wind. Arriving at a cornerstone in your life can push you over the edge if you are not ready psychologically to accept what is happening.

My spirit yearns to be in church where I can regroup. I can find a skilled psychiatrist to walk me through my situation while I lie on a couch staring up at the ceiling. No way. A psychiatrist is not skilled enough to counsel me. Church is where I am going for refuge.

There are disbelievers who argue God is not real. They debate over everything from creation to the evolution of man from dirt. Documentation is found in Genesis. And I am a believer. I will say this. In this wild and crazy world, I am shocked anyone can survive without a Higher Power.

I will go to church on any day of the week. I will attend a Baptist Church, a Catholic Church, a Methodist Church, a Jehovah Witness Church, a Pentecostal Church, a church on the corner, or a church under a tent. I enjoy the atmosphere and the music.

I am not an overly religious woman. I most certainly do not try to force my beliefs and values on anyone else. A person can believe whatever their heart desires. They do not have to answer to me. I do not have to pay their bills. They do not owe me an explanation for their actions. And I most definitely don't have a heaven or hell waiting for anyone.

There are Christians who try to force their religion on others. I hate it when I am going in a store, and a man or woman stops me to talk about a pamphlet. The worst part is when they finish their discussion they always ask for a small donation.

I am going to church today even though it is Saturday. Saturday is a perfect day to be in church. I have not proclaimed any religion. Seventh-Day Adventists attend church on Saturday. Baptist attends church on Sunday. Is the day important?

I may even force myself out of bed tomorrow on Sunday. I will go again. A double dose of religion will do me some good.

I have heard many Christians proclaim Jesus will soon return. If this is true, I say come this very second Jesus. I am tired of battling with life. It never fails. As soon as I overcome one struggle, another appears to defeat me.

I have to decide what to wear. I will more than likely wear my black skirt and brown blouse with a pair of black stockings and black high heel shoes. I am not a diva when going to church. On the flip side, I have seen my share of divas in the church. I wonder if they iron their outfits the night before to make sure it is perfect. I bet church divas get their dresses dry-cleaned.

It is okay to dress like a diva when going to church just leave the big hats at home. A small hat to accent an outfit is more than enough. A huge hat with rhinestones is too much. Those big hats block the view of other churchgoers. It is uncomfortable sitting behind a woman wearing a big hat in church.

There is this woman in church who makes it very annoying to sit behind her. You know the woman who stands up every chance she gets. If the collection plate is being passed around, she stands. If the choir is singing a song, she stands. If the pastor raises his voice during the sermon, she stands. This type of woman stands for everything.

This reminds me. I was at a Pentecostal Church across town. I sat on the left side, five rows from the front. I had a ball that day in church. Forgive me for being so blunt. I could not see very well because the woman in front of me was standing for almost the entire sermon waving her hands in the air. I focused my attention on what else was going on around me in the church.

I watched a man who was two rows away. He went to sleep after the pastor started preaching. It did not take very long before his mouth was open, and his eye glasses were sliding down his nose. Sitting next to him were two heavy-set ladies who thought they were sneaking into their purses eating candy.

I looked around the church to see what else was going on while the pastor was preaching. I saw children sleeping, adults whispering, couples giving each other the eye, and deacons monitoring the younger crowd on the second floor.

I didn't overlook Miss America. Every church has a lady who thinks she is Miss America. At this particular church, I spotted Miss America right away. She wore a big hat, short skirt with a jacket, nicely polished fingernails, and decorated pumps. She left her seat a couple of times to go somewhere. I knew she had to be Miss America in this church; all eyes were on her whenever she moved.

I wonder if Miss America ever suffers from a fatigued body. My body is changing. The stress is causing my legs to ache. My knees hurt. The back of my calves are sore. I have not been exercising enough to cause any of this, so I know these symptoms are being caused by stress.

When stress overwhelms me, my nerves get really frigidity. My hands shake. I get anxious. My stomach tends to make me regret not taking better care of myself. And how can I forget to mention the severe diarrhea?

Diarrhea is a monster. It does whatever it wants to do. When I get diarrhea, I literally have to live in the bathroom.

When I was a teenager, I took laxatives to stay regular or have a soft bowel movement. An older lady told me many years ago, "Take a laxative at least once a month. This will prevent your stomach from getting big." She is right. My stomach does appear to become smaller after I take laxatives. I do not need any assistance from Ex-Lax these days. My body is taking care of that department.

Church starts at eleven a.m. The pastors at all churches begin preaching around Noon or twelve-thirty. On the first Sunday, the pastor is usually late starting his sermon due to communion.

I stay in bed a bit longer thinking and contemplating what I will do to make myself useful today. I can go to church, get something to eat after church is over, and drop by to see Desiree. It all depends on what mood I am in after church service is over.

I doze off. I am awakened by a knock at my door. I rub my eyes to correct my vision. I remain in bed listening for another knock. I am not expecting any guests. Let whoever it is knock forever.

The clock reads nine forty-seven a.m. I might as well start getting dressed for church. I throw the sheets back, and raise my body from the bed, another day ahead of me. Am I ready? The answer is no. Regardless of what I am feeling, I have to press on.

The knocking has stopped. Whoever it was got the hint. It is impolite to go to someone's house without calling in advance. Patrick has a key. Desiree would scream my name until I opened the door. My mother would do the same. Whoever it was came without an invitation.

My pink slippers are waiting for me on the floor beside my bed. I slide my feet into my pink slippers then pause. They are so soft. My next stop is the bathroom. These legs are getting worse. I know I do not have arthritis. I am too young to have arthritis. Could it be a blood clot? I am not a diabetic. If my legs do not get better soon, I will go see my doctor.

I walk into the bathroom to find my clothes from yesterday on the floor. I kick them in the corner to give myself enough space to move around. I will put them away later. This is the glory of not having a husband and children. I am the messy one around here. I can be messy. I do not have to answer to anyone.

My shower cap is almost ready to retire. It still has the navy blue color with the yellow flowers. The elastic, however, is gone. I will buy another shower cap from the drugstore.

In the meantime, I will use this shower cap to protect my hair from getting wet. I put the shower cap on my head. I have to use a hair pen to tighten it in the front. I have to be creative. Think about the days when a shower cap was a luxury. They were expensive, and only the rich could afford them. What did ladies do in those days? They were creative.

I move the shower curtains and turn on the shower. I do not take bubble baths in the bathtub. I have to do to much work when sitting in a bathtub. I prefer showers. The hot water massages my body. Most ladies take baths in the bathtub. I am not impressed by bubble baths or fancy shower gels. They all make me itch. I am very sensitive between my legs. I have to be careful with all soaps containing perfumes. This is why I prefer to shower with Dove or Caress. They both wash away easily not leaving much residue on the skin.

My boyfriend tries to convince me to soak in the bathtub with bath beads and cute soaps. I refuse. The idea is to be clean and odor-free not itchy and frustrated.

I step into the shower placing my body directly underneath the warm water. What a relief it is.

After standing here for a few seconds, I use my washcloth to wash the important areas. I wash my back with a back brush. I allow the water to rinse away any soap. I am finished. I turn the shower off. My towel is hanging on the rack not to far away. Instead of stepping from the shower and wetting the rugs, I position myself closer to the rack to reach the towel.

I dry my face. The face has to be treated differently than the rest of the body. I have special masks, scrubs, and creams I place on my face. I did not bother to use any of them this morning.

I dry the remainder of my body then my feet. Although I know my feet are clean because I washed them, I still prefer to dry them last.

My usual routine goes into effect: hang the towel; put in my contact lenses; rub on some deodorant; lotion my body; brush my teeth; then leave the bathroom.

My hair is already styled. My friend, Tracy, does my hair whenever she is not busy with other clients. She does hair from her home. I told her she needs to get a booth in a hair salon. Her work is comparable to other beauticians working in a hair salon. She would have a lot of customers because everywhere I go somebody wants to know who does my hair.

Into the bedroom I rush! In the closet, I have my clothes organized by pants, shirts, skirts, dresses, jackets, and so forth. I go to the very rear of my closet to get a two-piece skirt set. The color is dark purple and white, nothing to brag about. I do not have to iron this outfit. I changed my mind about wearing the black skirt and brown blouse.

As I take each item from the hanger, I slip it on my body. Wait a minute, I forgot my undergarments. What am I thinking? I remove my clothes and put on a purple bra with dark blue underwear. Okay, do not frown on me. We all have our days. The colors do not match. I then get dressed in my outfit.

To finish, I go inside of the drawer and get my stockings. I re-enter the closet to put on a pair of black high heel shoes. My make-up case is in the drawer beneath my hair accessories. In five minutes top, I whip on face powder, a touch of blush, and purple lipstick.

I give myself a wink of reassurance before I spray on some perfume. It is to late for body powder.

Not wanting to waste another second, I walk into the living room to find my purse and car keys. This place is a total mess. I have to do some cleaning soon. I drop by the kitchen to drink a big glass of orange juice. My appetite is gone. I am not hungry.

Out the door I go. The neighborhood kids are playing. They are riding their bikes. I envy their innocence and happiness.

Cassandra is not in her chair. This is unlike her. She is somewhere doing something sneaky. Cassandra stays in mischief.

I had better not question her whereabouts? Knowing Cassandra she will read my mind and race to my car to hold a conversation.

I walk over to my car, click the alarm box on the key ring, and pull on the car door. I get inside. Switching on the ignition starts the car, the air conditioner, and the radio. It is eleven-ten a.m.

I place my car in reverse. I reverse from my parking space. The gear has to be changed to D for Drive. I am ready to go.

At the second light, I turn left. The light turns red. I hear music coming from the radio. Oh, I like this song. I forgot the name of it. I know some of the lyrics. When I first heard this song, I cried. The words made me cry. The artist sings about love. She is singing about a woman who meets her husband, a friend, and a lover. This is exactly what my bruised heart has wanted for many years. Instead, I am with a man who swears he is God's gift to women.

As the song plays on, I speed to the church. The church is not far from my apartment. There are more than enough churches in the city of Louisville. There is no way a person can say they do not have a church to attend. It is impossible.

When the clock strikes eleven thirty-four a.m., I pull into the gate surrounding the church. Of course, there are no available parking spaces in sight. I drive around. On the opposite side of the entrance gate, I find a park. I have to walk further than I would like. No complaints from me. I can use the exercise.

I park my car. The radio and the air conditioner both stop as the car keys are removed from the ignition. Although I am on church property, I put my club on the steering wheel. A thief has no conscience. Remember, the pastor tells us, "Sinners are welcome." This means thieves attend church as well. They will steal a car from a church or anywhere else to go joy riding. We are living in bad times. Thieves have no shame especially if they are addicted to drugs.

I step from inside of my car. A small Mitsubishi parks behind me. The windows are tinted. I cannot see the driver. There is a law in this state against tinted windows being to dark. I know one thing for sure. They are not in a parking space. They have to move their car when the church service is over. I should not have to wait around for them to move.

Before long, a tall man steps from the passenger side of the car holding an infant. Then a young woman gets out of the driver's side. She is extremely tall to be a woman. She has to be 6'3". She is tall and skinny. I assume they are married. How sweet. All I have ever asked for is what they appear to have.

My boyfriend is somewhere asleep. I know his pattern. He sleeps late on Saturday and Sunday.

I have tried to get my boyfriend to come to

church with me. He has every excuse in the book for not going to church. I do not pressure him anymore. His excuses are unbearable. He has to live for himself. I refuse to try to raise a grown man. That is his mother's job.

While walking toward the church, I see this young man wearing a baby blue suit. His shirt is multicolored, and he has on a big chain. The fashion police would arrest him. His shoes are aqua blue. And I ask myself, "Where on earth does he think he is going?"

I notice a sign that reads, Youth Revival — Join us —. The church members have fancy cars. These are some expensive cars they are driving, I think to myself as I continue walking towards the entrance of the church.

At the door, I pull it to let myself inside. Inside the church, the entrance area is empty, excluding the deacons who are on the sofa talking. They ignore me as I pass them.

I direct myself to a seat inside of the congregation. Up front, a man is singing. He sings, "Let it shine on me. Let the Light House shine on me..." His voice rings across the church. The piano and drums play in the background. The singer stops singing after the speaker gives him a signal with his hands.

The speaker standing at the pulpit challenges the young people in the church to make a sacrifice. I think he wants them to attend church more often. This gentleman is the speaker for Divine Worship. He is giving an extended message about peer pressure.

"We must learn to focus on our youth," he says. "Our youth should be educated and motivated. Many will never take advice. There are a handful of youth who will not be saved," he goes on to say.

If Desiree had only given our mother a chance, their relationship would not be so strained. They were always arguing. Since my sister contracted HIV, their relationship has improved. The anger in all of us has to stop. The past belongs in the past. There is no way we can prepare for the future while trying to correct what has happened in the past. What we did or said to hurt each other in the past should stay in the past. This is a new day with new triumphs.

I sit here in church listening. I hope the youth are listening. They do not realize what lies ahead for them.

As the speaker finalizes his message, the piano

player switches songs. The drum player joins. The speaker acknowledges the pastor by giving him the microphone.

"Amen congregation. Let's give our brother a round of applause. Praise God for using him. We are now at a crucial point in our service. For all of you who have strayed from the church, we want to invite you to come home. Don't be left in the pigpen," the pastor tells the congregation.

This sounds like the benediction. Did they start early? I thought the pastor preaches from Noon to one o'clock.

A woman wearing a flowered dress with matching shoes heads to the front. A man follows her. Three more people join them. The congregation claps as they make their way down to the front. I think I have missed something. It sounds to me like church is over.

The pastor speaks again, "Set an example for the children. Teach them. Father we ask for blessings for our young people. We pray the youth live in an environment of love and Christian compassion. God help our youth recognize you as their Savior and Guide. We pray for them all. Continue to touch their lives. God we remember those who are sick and shut-in. We know you have all power. Whatever our needs are today, Lord teach us and grant it to us in your grace, Amen."

I'll be darn. The service is over. Something is wrong here. After the pastor prays, the congregation sits down again. As the deacons and deaconesses move through the aisles of the church, I slip out the door. I walk over to a deacon.

"Did service finish early today?"

"Yes. We are having Culture Day. Why don't you join us under the tent for a home cooked meal?"

"I better not. I am on a diet."

"Sorry to hear that young lady. We have enough food for us all."

"I am not hungry. I can get food from a restaurant. I wanted to hear the pastor preach."

"Well, you can always come to Wednesday Night Prayer Meeting."

"Church folk eat to much," I mumble under my breath.

"Excuse me. Did you say something young lady?"

"No!"

Chapter Eleven

Coming to church today did nothing for me spiritually. I wanted to hear the pastor. I came in during the benediction. Divine worship should not be shortened to have a feast. If the people want to eat, they should have enough self-control to wait until after the sermon. And the Bible does teach us gluttony is a sin.

Listen to me. Can you believe I am passing judgment? Here I am with skeletons in my closest. I should be the last person walking around looking down on others. If someone were to open my closet, a bunch of skeletons would jump out. I have so many skeletons in my closet they are ready to force their way out. I laugh to myself while heading towards the exit.

I am sure the man heard my smart remark. Why does human nature make us respond to a rude individual by saying, "Excuse me!" Why don't we just tell them what we think about them and get on with life?

I have to walk back through the entrance area to exit the church. There are tables against the corner containing information about the church calendar, the church daycare center, and a tutoring program being offered to high school students by the church. Personally, I think a church is more effective when the church is open everyday of the week. This gives the church members a place to go during the week and on the Sabbath.

Also, parents won't have to worry about their kids being on the street corner. They can take them to church. While there, the parent can get involved by volunteering with a missionary group. The church is a Band-Aid for the wounded. Churchgoers require more than worship on the Sabbath to keep them going.

I exit the church and walk to my car. The

parking lot is crowded with cars. Everyone is not going to the tent to eat. Some members are leaving.

Just as I thought. The couple who parked their car behind mine has not moved their car. I bet they are somewhere underneath the tent stuffing their faces.

I really do not want to wait here for them to move their car. Maybe I should go find them. In the event I do find them, I will let them know they did not park in a parking space. Why inconvenience me? That's what the world is lacking — basic consideration.

To prevent an argument and a potential fight at the church, I might as well go ahead and sit inside my car. This was a total waste. I could have stayed home in bed for this headache. I wish I had known ahead of time what was on the church's calendar for today. Most likely, I would have driven to Mt. Bethel CMA Baptist Church.

I roll down my car windows to allow a breeze to blow in. I am not in a rush to go anywhere. I can wait.

I have the patience of a lamb. Anyone else would find the couple instead of waiting for them.

I, on the other hand, will test myself to see how long I can wait here before getting upset and searching for them. Patience is a virtue.

The pastor of this church delivers a dynamic message. He brings the house down. I prefer old-fashioned preaching. When a preacher reads from notes, they lose my interest. A pastor should not have to read from notes while at the pulpit. They should already know what they are going to say.

A professional lecturer does not read from notes. They practice their presentation until they know what to say. A pastor, of all people, should know better.

Like the old saying goes, "Many are called, but few are chosen." This statement is true. Every pastor is not ordained by God.

I think a pastor is unique by the way they walk, talk, and live. A pastor does not have to impress with their dress attire or fancy cars. There has to be a spark to them even before they utter a word.

I am not impressed by pastors who wear big rings on their fingers. It reminds me of a pimp. A pimp wears big rings on his fingers with flashy clothes. A pastor should have nothing in common with a pimp.

I want to share a secret with you. I had the biggest crush on a pastor as a child. I wanted him to be my husband. I never told anybody about my crush. I knew they would laugh. I assume I was around nine or ten-years-old. He was a handsome, single pastor. All the ladies in the church wanted to be his wife.

I recall wearing my white dress to church. All the ladies wore white on Ladies Day. My white dress flowed around the legs. It was a dress designed for a child.

On one particular Ladies Day, the pastor asked all ladies in the church who wanted a husband to form a line. I thought he was asking all the ladies who wanted to marry him to get in a line. I shyly stood behind Sister Morgan.

The entire congregation laughed at me when I got to the front of the line to speak with the pastor. They thought I was joking around. He even laughed. He took my girlish love for granted. From that day on, my love for him faded. I was smart enough to know a man who loves you does not shame you in front of an entire congregation of people.

I sit here, waiting for the couple to move their

car. I will sit. I will wait. They will come eventually. I know food is a temptation for most of us, but being full triggers us to move away from the table.

I have a plan. I will wait here for an hour. If they do not come within an hour, I will find them. An hour is long enough to eat and be merry.

Chapter Twelve

The clock is ticking. Where are they? Nobody can eat that much. Eat and be done with it. Do not hang around the table waiting for a second serving of food. That's the trouble with America today. We overindulge with everything. This is why we have the highest rates of obesity in the nation.

Children everywhere are obese. They are suffering from diabetes, heart disease, high blood pressure, and high cholesterol. This is terrible because kids are now dying from diet-related diseases, which can be prevented. Public Health professionals are targeting adolescence to change their diets before it is to late. And it is a proven fact high-priority health risk behaviors begin during adolescence and continue into adulthood.

Cardiovascular disease starts during childhood and worsens with age. I was reading a national survey called the YRBSS. This acronym stands for Youth Risk Behavior Surveillance Survey. The survey is conducted in all fifty states. The purpose of this study is to monitor youth behavior to determine what can be done to educate them about their risky behavior.

Public schools and health agencies can use the information provided in the YRBSS to better prepare youth for the future. By reading the YRBSS, I discovered many of our youth are not very concerned about their health. They are smoking cigarettes and marijuana. They are having unprotected sex and getting pregnant. The cases of HIV and AIDS in ages ten to twenty-five have skyrocketed.

I look at the clock then glance through my rear view mirror. The couple is nowhere in sight. Their car is still blocking mine. I can't leave. I am stuck here.

I have sat here for forty-five minutes waiting

patiently for them to arrive. I think I will be forced to give them a piece of my mind when they get here. The driver knew she was not parking in a parking space. Common sense should have told her to move her car after the service was over.

I can sit here for fifteen minutes waiting for them to come, or I can do the next best thing; find them. Fifteen minutes will make an hour. An hour is long enough for them to sit around eating.

I roll up my car windows. I will leave my purse here until I return. I shouldn't be gone long. I slam my car door shut.

I am going to look for them. It will take about fifteen minutes to find them. This means I did wait an hour after all.

I walk through the parking lot on my way to the tent located on the west side of the church's parking lot. Before I reach the tent, I smell food. It smells like a mixture of chicken and pound cake. I love pound cake especially with cream cheese baked in with the ingredients.

My face is frowned, and I am walking fast. In between my frustration, I lick my lips. It would not hurt my diet if I eat a slice of pound cake.

I squeeze through two cars. These two cars are parked so close. I can barely get my hips through this small space. I walk sideways to get through. I am getting closer to the tent. I walk ahead with fever in my steps.

The tent is huge. I see tables with enough food to feed an army, so this is how they celebrate around here.

The children are running around the tent splashing in puddles of water from rain earlier this morning. The adults are eating and being merry. Some of the ladies have on aprons. They must be serving the food.

I do not see the couple. I know they are somewhere around here. I stand here watching and waiting until I see them. All of the tables are numbered. Sure enough, at table number eight, there they are.

I attempt to smile as I walk over to the table. The woman is now holding the baby. The man is to busy eating to notice what's happening around him. This entire tent could fall on his head, and he would not notice.

"Hi, how are you doing?"

"I'm fine," she says and looks at me wondering who I am.

"You parked your car behind mine. I have been waiting for an hour to leave."

"I am so sorry. I didn't know."

"That's alright."

"Tyson, hold the baby. I have to move the car."

"Wait a second. Let me clean my hands."

"Hurry, Tyson. We are blocking this lady's car."

This man is a pig. He has barbecue sauce all around his mouth. Barbecue is not a messy food. I can tell he eats like a slob.

He gets the baby. The woman walks with me to our cars. We hold a conversation while walking.

"I am so sorry. It's so hard being a new mother. I can't remember anything. And my husband is no help."

"Congratulations on your baby," I respond.

There are so many things I can say to this lady. The demon in me tells me to curse her, or hurt her feelings for parking behind me. The angel in me tells me to be kind. I will hold my peace. It could have been worse.

Once we get to our cars, she apologizes to me again then moves her car. I get inside of my car and drive to the gate to exit the parking lot. The traffic has slowed down. Those people who were in a rush left right after the pastor did the benediction.

At the gate, I make a right turn. I will drop by Desiree's house to check on her. I did not speak to her before I came to church. I bet she is pacing the floors crying or worrying herself sick.

I have asked Desiree not to cry in front of her two children. Her daughter is six-years-old, and her son is two-years-old. The kids are smart enough to sense something is wrong with their mother. They should not be subjected to her constant crying. She has to be strong for them. When they become teenagers, we can explain AIDS and HIV to them. Right now, they would not understand the grief we are all feeling.

My sister does not live far from the church. Louisville is not a big city. I can fill my tank on Sunday, and I will have enough gas to take me until Thursday or Friday.

The neighborhood around this church is going down to the dumps. Men are hanging on the corner selling drugs. Kids have to walk on the opposite side of the street to avoid them. I even see bums gathering across the street under the big oak tree. We never had bums in this city until a new train station was built some years ago. The Mayor and City Council voted to build the new train station as a way of bringing more revenue into Louisville. The train has brought in more revenue. Also, it has brought in more unexpected residents, which could eventually increase our crime rate.

It is so hot and humid outside. The heat from the bright sun makes most residents in Louisville uneasy. And no one seems to be happy due to the humidity.

I see a dog lying on the side of the road as I turn the curve. Some dummy has crushed the poor animal. A bone is exposed. Blood and skin are pressed into the street. The guts are everywhere. This animal will stay here until the rain comes along to wash its' remains down the sewer.

I am almost at my sister's house. I look through my rear view mirror to see a woman driving a burgundy car. She is tailgating. I am not in a rush. She can go around me. I drive at a steady pace ignoring her.

All of a sudden, she swerves around me. She has pulled her car next to mine. Her car is close to the passenger side of my car. I roll the window all the way down on the passenger side of my car.

"You are driving below the speed limit," she yells.

"Really," I say.

"Yes, really. Are you stupid or what?"

"Honey, get a life." I keep my eyes on the road.

"No, you get a life. Pull over. Say it to my face," she tells me in frustration.

"Sweetie, I have bigger fish to fry. I just left church, somewhere you need to be. Have a nice day." I drive on ignoring her.

She is still screaming and yelling profanities at me. I blow my horn at her then smile. This has to be her lucky day. If I had not gone to church, I would have shown her I can use profanity better than she does. Road rage strikes again.

I can hear her blowing her horn at me. I thought she was in a rush. I was wrong. She is wasting valuable time harassing me. Life is too short for this childish behavior. I could pull over and fight. What would I gain? My sister needs me.

I drive into the next lane. She recognizes I am ignoring her. She drives away.

I am worried about my sister. I refuse to allow a total stranger to ruin my day. She has to keep her misery to herself. I am not about to allow her to rent any space in my brain.

I am on Jupiter Creek Road. My sister is not far from here. I listen to my radio until I pull my car into Desiree's driveway.

At Desiree's house, I turn off my car. I place the club on the steering wheel then lock it. My purse is lying on the passenger's seat. I retrieve my purse and throw it on my shoulder while preparing to walk up the sidewalk.

I see my niece sitting on the porch. She is crying. Her hair is combed in two ponytails. She is wearing blue jeans with a white T-shirt. Oh no! What is happening?

"Cleopatra, why are you crying, baby?"

"My mommy is sick."

"She is not sick, Cleopatra. Your mommy is having some trouble with her health. She will be alright soon." I regret having to lie to her.

The door leading into Desiree's house is

opened wide. A stray dog or cat could be inside hiding. A snake can crawl through the front door.

"Stay here while I go see your mommy."

"Okay, Auntie."

Before getting completely inside the house, I smell a nasty odor. It is the garbage can. The odor strikes my nostrils. It smells like old pork. You know how pork smells when it rots? Pork cannot remain in a kitchen garbage can for more than a day. Depending on the temperature in the house, if left sitting long enough, pork smells like a decayed body.

Desiree does not clean her house anymore. My mother and I clean for her whenever we get the chance. It is a mess in here. Clothes are everywhere. Shoes are on the couch. Dishes are piled in the kitchen sink. The closet doors are hanging from the hinges. Something has to give with my sister.

I walk around in the house. I go into my sister's bedroom. She is on the bed crying with the blanket pulled over her head.

"Desiree, what is going on?"

"I am hurting so bad. You just don't know."

"What is hurting? Is it your chest?"

"No, I am hurting all over."

"Do you want to go to the Emergency Room? Get dressed. We can go to the Emergency Room."

"Don't worry. There is no reason to go to the hospital. They can't do anything for me."

"You are sick. They can give you a shot or some medicine."

"My doctor already gave me some medicine. I have been vomiting all day. The medicine is to strong."

"Did you eat?"

"I tried to eat earlier. I can't hold anything in my stomach."

"Well, this is why you are sick."

It hurts me to see her in this condition. My sister breaks down and starts crying. I hold my own tears. I can cry later.

"I keep asking God for an answer. Why me? Why me?" My sister's lips tremble as she speaks.

"Desiree, you can't question God. You have to ask him to tell you what to do next."

"It has been rough for me all of my life. Why is this happening to me?"

She cries even harder. I want to hug her, but I cannot build the courage to touch my sister. I sit beside her on the bed to comfort her.

"You have to keep yourself healthy. If you continue acting this way, you won't see your kids become adults. You can live longer than me. Life is so uncertain."

"I am not going to live longer than you, and you know it!"

"Come on, Desiree. Pull yourself together."

"God knows I have asked Him to forgive me for everything I have ever done wrong in my life. I wasn't perfect. I made mistakes." Desiree says.

"We have all made mistakes. Everybody does not tell what they go through, but believe me we have all had our share of ups-and-downs."

"But I have two kids."

Cleopatra walks into the bedroom. She makes a couple of sobbing noises. Her face looks swollen. "Cleopatra, go outside. Let Auntie finish talking to your mommy."

She leaves the bedroom. I think she wants to know if her mother is okay. She does not know what to think. Her little mind is confused. She only knows her mother is crying.

"Look at your daughter. You should not let her see you cry. Cry behind closed doors. Wait until they are in school and the daycare. You have to get stronger for your kids."

"I know. I am doing my best."

My sister continues crying. "Why me? Why me?"

I wish I could give her an answer. Why anyone is the question. Why do hundreds of victims contract the virus? Why do half of them die in less than three years? I do not know why. Only God knows why. My heart is heavy as my grandmother use to say.

"Have you spoken to Robert?"

"He won't return my calls. I sent him an email. He is not answering his telephone. He has Caller ID. He knows it is me."

"He is not going to call you or return your calls. Isn't he sick?"

"Yeah, somebody told me they saw him. They said he has lost a lot of weight."

"He is dying, Desiree."

Robert is dying. He has given my sister HIV,

and he is dying. There is no way he did not know he was infected. He is keeping a low profile these days. The word is getting around he has the virus.

Why did I ever mention Robert's name? After my sister hears his name, she starts crying uncontrollably.

Desiree keeps a bedpan next to her bed. She uses it to vomit in. She grabs the bedpan and tries to vomit. A clear, watery liquid comes from her throat.

Tears and mucous are spread all over her face. She is frightening me. I stand. I walk into the kitchen to get a paper towel from the counter. I take the paper towel back to Desiree in the bedroom. She wipes her nose.

I am not afraid to be around my sister. They say the virus can be transmitted from body fluids. If I must die, let it not be in vain, let it be with my sister. I have not done very much research on the virus, yet I refuse to treat my sister like she is contaminated. I will go into the grave with her.

My mother and I have to convince Desiree to allow a nurse to visit her during the week. A nurse with knowledge about HIV can tell us what to do.

Until we hire a nurse, I will stand by my sister

through thick and thin.

"Shanna, go home. Leave me alone. I want to go to sleep."

"What about the kids?"

"They will be fine. My kids are my only reason for being here."

Her statement switches on a light bulb in my head. I hope Desiree is not thinking about suicide. I know she did tell me she would kill herself and her kids. She said her kids would go to heaven, and she would go to hell.

"Why don't we go see a movie? Let's get something to eat. Let's go somewhere, anywhere besides this house. Don't you want some fresh air?"

"No, I am waiting on my answer from God."

I really do not know what answer she is talking about. Is God supposed to tell her there will be brighter days ahead? Is God supposed to tell her she will not die? What is God supposed to tell her?

"Can I use your telephone? I have to call Mama." I say to Desiree.

Desiree does not move. I know she heard me. I go over to the dresser to get the telephone. I dial my mother's number. She does not answer. Where can she be? I place the telephone on the receiver. Speak of the devil. I hear my mother's voice in the front yard. What a relief.

My mother comes into the bedroom to join my sister and me. My mother looks around the room before making a comment.

"Desiree, you have to get out of this bed. Do something else," Mother says.

"Something else like what?"

"You can clean this house for starters. You can cook for your children. You can take a bath."

"Not now, Mama. I will do it later."

"You better get out of this bed. How do you expect to stay healthy acting this way?"

My mother is upset. Her eyes are bulging. They always bulge when she gets upset.

My sister starts crying again. Her tears are painful for me. Her tears are coming from her soul. She still can't believe this has happened to her. I still can't believe it myself. We are all in a state of disbelief.

"Shanna, I have some groceries in the trunk. Help me bring them inside." My mother beckons me to leave the room.

"Where are your car keys?"

"Right here."

My mother and I go outside to her car to get the groceries. We bring the groceries inside placing them in the kitchen. Cleopatra puts the groceries away.

My mother and I stay to clean Desiree's house. Before we leave to go home, my sister walks into the living room with the blanket gripped to her chest.

"Thank you all."

"Oh girl, please. I have always cleaned behind you ever since you were a baby. This is a mother's duty," my mother tells Desiree. There is so much love in my mother's eyes when she looks at Desiree.

My mother then walks out the door. I can tell she is ready to cry. I want to cry. My eyes are getting watery. I had better leave.

CHAPTER THIRTEEN

My mother leaves Desiree's house before me. I kiss my niece and nephew on the cheek before I head to my car.

"Auntie, can I go with you?" my niece asks me.

"No sweetheart. Your mommy needs you to stay here."

"Alright," she looks disappointed.

"Cleopatra, make sure your brother does not leave the yard."

"Yes, Auntie."

"I will call to check on you all later."

"Bye, Auntie," Cleopatra says to me. My nephew reaches out his arms for me to pick him up. I bend over, and give him another kiss on his forehead.

I walk to the front yard. I get into my car. I remove the club and drive away. I make it around the corner before I burst into tears. I am not sure what to do or where to go. This can't be happening to our family. Not my family.

I cry all the way home. I know other drivers on the road are staring at me. Who cares? They to will have tragedy strike their family someday. Then they will be able to understand me.

Patrick is not here. I do not see his truck. He is somewhere with another woman. The nerve of the man. He is never here when I need him most.

I exit my car and enter my apartment. I did not leave any windows open before I left this morning. It is hot in here. I walk over to the air conditioner to switch it on.

I grab the remote control for the television in my living room. I turn the channels until I find a movie. I will watch a movie to clear my head.

I walk into my bedroom to undress. I throw all of my clothes on the bed. I put my shoes in the closet. I put on a nightgown then go into the kitchen. This kind of pressure makes me crave sweets. I want to eat something sweet.

Inside the freezer, I have a pint of Rocky Road Ice Cream. I am going to eat all of it. I get myself a big spoon then walk into the living room. I fall down on my couch. This has to do for now.

I dig into the ice cream while watching the movie. I do not recognize this movie. It has to be a new release on *WTKI* Channel 11.

In the movie, there is this female character that is following a man who has her friend in his van. I think her friend is already dead. The movie is not making a lot of sense. Instead of following the man, she should be contacting the police. She has a knife. A knife will not stop this man. He is big enough to take the knife from her.

Moviemakers know what they are doing when they create movies with such suspense. They create movies to involve the viewers. I am here eating ice cream, yelling at the television, and trying not to think about my sister.

The man in the movie is going around a curve on a mountain. It is foggy. Their cars are the only two cars on this isolated mountainside.

He notices she is following him. He speeds up.

She speeds up. He drives ahead. She pursues him. Then he stops. She stops. This has to be a game of cat and mouse.

He waits for her to pass him. She keeps her position. "Go around me," he tells her. She waits. He starts to drive again. She starts to follow him. I do not know how much more of this I can stand. I do not know what will happen next. There is a great deal of suspense in this movie.

I watch on as he drives into an electric gate. I assume this is his house. She has to park outside the gate. She actually thinks he has not seen her.

A commercial interrupts the movie. I go to the kitchen to dump the empty ice cream container in the garbage. I have to drink a glass of water to get rid of the chocolate taste from my mouth. Rocky Road Ice Cream has chocolate covered nuts, fudge, marshmallow swirls, and milk chocolate ice cream. Let's not discuss the calorie count.

I have to use the bathroom before the movie comes back on. I drink the water and place the cup in the kitchen sink. A new commercial is on. I use the bathroom, wash my hands, and then return to my couch. The movie should be on shortly.

I stretch on the couch. My legs are shorter than the couch. This makes it more comfortable for me. My nightgown is silk with a split on the side. I pull my nightgown down. It moves whenever I move on the couch.

The movie is on. This lady is at the electric gate deciding how she will get inside. She has to think of an intelligent plan. The electric gate is tall.

I am a bit sleepy. I get sleepy whenever I am depressed. I get fatigued and tired when depression comes over me. I will watch as much of the movie as I can until I fall asleep.

I watch more of the movie to see what she will do next. This has to be a movie. In real life, a friend would not follow a killer to a remote mountain to rescue the body of a dead friend.

As I assumed, I fall asleep. In my sleep, I have a dream. I dream an angel is holding my hand. The angel is surrounded by a bright light. There are no wings on the angel. I am unable to see the face. I can see a white robe and nothing more. In my dream, I allow the angel to guide me. We walk across the clouds. Smoke appears to be covering our feet. I am struggling to hold on to the angel.

And without warning, I step on the wrong cloud and fall from the sky. I yell as my body crushes against the wind.

"No. Don't let me fall. Catch me. Please." I awaken from my own screams.

What is the significance of this dream? Satan is playing tricks on me. He wants me to think God has forgotten my family.

I sit up on the couch. I wipe across my eyes. It was only a dream. I try to convince myself. It is not real.

I will call Desiree and my mother soon. My boyfriend did not leave any messages for me. Where is he? I get my telephone, and dial his cellular phone. He answers.

"Where are you?"

"Well, good afternoon to you."

"Skip the junk. Where are you?" I demand in a grouchy tone.

"I am in Michigan."

"Michigan"

"My boss called me last night. He asked me to get here as soon as possible."

"Is there an emergency?" I ask him.

"No. He asked me to sit in for him at the annual conference."

"Annual conference. You have to be joking."

"I tried to call you last night. The line was busy all night."

"I knocked it off the hook by mistake. Did you try my cellular phone?"

"I didn't have time."

"You don't seem to have much time for me lately. Is there something I should know?"

"Such as..." Patrick asks me with a puzzled voice.

"Are you cheating on me?"

"Shanna, let's not go through this over the phone. We can talk when I get home."

"When will you get back?"

"I will be there on Monday night."

"Would you have called me if I hadn't called you?" I ask Patrick.

"You know I was going to call, so what's up?"

"Nothing much"

"You sound tired. You sick?"

"No, I am not sick, Patrick."

"Why the squeaky voice?"

"I will talk to you when you get here."

"Shanna, don't hang up."

"Why not? You didn't respect me enough to call me. I am tired of you hurting me. I can do better than this."

"I see where this is going. Hold that thought until I am in front of you. There is nothing I can do while here in Michigan. I am going to the hotel tonight, and sleep until tomorrow."

"Oh, so you are imitating Sleeping Beauty and the Seven Dwarfs. Enjoy yourself in Michigan while I am alone here in Louisville." I hang up the phone and take it off the hook.

I spend the remainder of the evening watching television, snacking, and talking to Desiree and my mother.

I do not speak to Patrick anymore tonight. He did not give me the telephone number to his hotel room. I know in my heart there is no hotel room. He is with another woman. It gets so lonely being here by myself.

CHAPTER FOURTEEN

I spent the remainder of the evening alone. While speaking to my mother and Desiree, I longed to hear Patrick's voice. Having a man around is different than confiding in family members.

Besides, Desiree was not very talkative. She only listened while I did all the talking. And mother was singing the same tune. Why can't she face the truth?

I am thinking about yesterday when I drove away from Desiree's house. I should have stayed. She asked me to leave, which is the only reason why I left her and the kids. It was not my choice.

I am getting weaker as the days go by. I thought

I was going to graduate from college and fulfill my dreams. Because everything is going so wrong with my family, I may have to put those dreams on hold. I am in no shape to study for my classes.

I am on the verge of exploding. I can't deal with anymore pressure. College is pressure. Studying for exams, doing research papers, and working on group projects is pressure. I am not ready to return to work. I am not stable enough mentally to remain in school. Where will I go from here?

The crying from Desiree, my own agony, watching my mother fall apart, are all sources of stress in my life. I am alive, but I am dead. I am a dead woman walking.

Anyone who has ever felt a tremendous amount of pain can relate to what I am going through. I am alive and breathing, but I am dead inside. Anybody who has not been tried and tested in the fire knows nothing about being a walking zombie.

Today is Sunday. I have no intentions of leaving my apartment. I thought I would be interested in going to church. I changed my mind. I went yesterday. My plan is to stay here in bed. This is where I am happiest. I plan to avoid having contact with anyone if they are not Desiree or my mother. The world would only upset me.

My friends have to deal with their own problems. I have not spoken to my friends very much since Desiree got sick. I just stopped calling them or returning their calls. I am not concerned with anything occurring outside of these four walls.

It is quiet in my bedroom. My boyfriend is in Michigan. I know he is not being faithful to me. He has women all over the United States. I should have told him to stay away from me. He did not even bother to ask about my sister during our phone conversation yesterday. He knows she is sick.

I remember the nights when I had to beg him to go home. He could not get enough of me. Now today, I have to beg him to stay with me. He treats me like a mistress.

I have to confess. I am disappointed about my sister's illness and the way Patrick is treating me. Although it is not his fault Desiree is sick, he could be more supportive of me. I would be satisfied knowing he cared.

Patrick wants to have his cake and eat it to. We

are consenting adults. It is not right for him to cause me so much grief. He has done mean things to me in the past. I forgave him. The mean things he is doing now will not be forgiven. He smiles in my face and stabs me in my back.

I have stood by his side waiting for our relationship to improve. Obviously, he has another agenda, which does not include me.

I refuse to spend my entire day questioning what I did wrong in our relationship. I am trying to save what we have before there is nothing left to save. Patrick is not trying to save what we have. His only concern is satisfying the woman he is sneaking around with.

I believe when two people stay in a relationship for more than one year they should move to the next level. The next level includes marriage, a family, and a home. These are some of the things I want for myself. Every woman wants to get married and have a family.

The older I get the more I want stability. I would be a total fool to stay in this relationship with no promises of a future. What if he drags me along for years then marries someone else? I will be devastated, not to mention being abandoned without any children.

I refuse to allow Patrick to continue coming and going whenever he pleases. We have never walked down the aisle and said, "I do." Nevertheless, I think the state of Kentucky accepts Common Law Marriages in court as an official marriage. We do live under the same roof, occasionally. Louisville, Kentucky most likely allows for Common Law Marriages.

I am going to put my foot down. I deserve some type of explanation. He demands I explain my whereabouts to him. Am I wrong for wanting the same respect?

This is not a donation center. I have no more donations to offer him. Christmas has come and gone. Santa Claus won't return until next year. His selfish behavior has to end.

I lie here in my bed with the sheets pulled over my head. I toss and turn from side to side beneath the sheets. My body has never been so achy. If I could, I would escape all of these problems.

The air conditioner works very well. It is freezing in this apartment. It is colder than a hospital. I like the cold air. The cold air rocks me to sleep.

Hospitals are cold because it prevents the spread of germs and bacteria, which is another reason why I can appreciate a freezing, cold air conditioner.

I will call Desiree to make sure she is not in bed while her children are destroying the place. Knowing Desiree, she is in the bed shedding crocodile tears. My sister acts so pathetic. She cries and cries until her ears hurt.

Desiree has been complaining of pain in her throat. I cannot bring myself to look at her throat. If I were to see her throat swollen, it would send me into a state of panic. I know HIV affects the thyroid glands. The thyroid glands get inflamed causing strep throat.

Desiree has sores in her mouth. The sores are on her tongue. They are white in color and lumpy almost like a cauliflower. The sores on the outside of her mouth resemble fever blisters. HIV can cause damage to the immune system. Desiree's mental function is not the same due to brain cell damage. Desiree was previously healthy before she got infected with HIV.

I have been saying I am going to the library to do my own personal research on HIV and AIDS. I have not gotten there yet. I will go soon. I want to know what is happening in my sister's body. I thought people with HIV did not get sick. I was under the impression sickness came when AIDS invaded the immune system. There are far too many misconceptions about HIV and AIDS.

I have seen commercials on television about AIDS. They suggest you can be working with someone who has AIDS and never know they have tested positive for the virus. I am aware AIDS is an infectious disease that has more victims in the African-American Community than in other communities.

AIDS has been around for many years. AIDS was a silent killer until so many people started to get infected, and the media started a frenzy. There is information everywhere about the virus; nevertheless, people are still ignorant to the facts. I know people like me who believed it would never touch my family. This is why I did not do any reading on the topic.

All I can say to people who may think they are untouchable is "BE CAREFUL". AIDS does not discriminate. There is no racism when it comes to AIDS. Always remember AIDS is colorblind.

Forget about prejudices. Never think you are to high or mighty. Anyone can contract the virus. The police may not be able to touch you. Man may not be able to touch you. You may think of yourself as being larger than life. I am here to tell you having an attitude like this is dangerous. No man, woman, boy, or girl is to far beyond the reach of AIDS.

It can happen to you. It can happen to your mother. It can happen to your father. The virus is deadly. An ignorant act of pleasure can bring a death sentence upon you. The man who infected my sister is attractive and handsome. He is every woman's knight in shining armor. Beneath his handsome demeanor, he is corrupt. In his penis rests the ability to kill, destroy, and cripple.

Take HIV and AIDS serious. The virus is floating around waiting for a warm body. Don't let your body become a home for HIV and AIDS. This is serious business.

My dear sister. When we were kids, we protected each other. When we had fights in school, we defended each other. We always fought together.

Even after we graduated from high school becoming adults, we kept our bond. She would defend me from anyone who wanted to do harm to me. Desiree would come to my rescue. My sister has always been my hero.

I can't help dying inside. I have failed Desiree. She needs me now? Why can't I save her? My bank account is a joke. I am not financially stable enough to buy my sister the expensive medicine she needs to survive. It hurts me because I am not in a position to help Desiree. Poor people and middle class people do not get the same medical treatment as upper class and rich people. Poor people have to practically volunteer to be guinea pigs in order to get necessary medical treatment.

I have a professor who was telling the class about a drug called the "cocktail". He says it is difficult to obtain this drug. This drug is expensive. He mentioned most AIDS patients cannot afford "cocktails".

Rich patients can afford to purchase "cocktails". My professor says he is sure this drug extends the lifespan.

I have heard mention of famous people

contracting the virus. When the media broadcasts a story about a famous person having the virus, America listens for a moment. Americans have sympathy for famous people. I heard about a famous sports player who has the virus. He is living a productive life. I realize AIDS is not just a story exploited by the news media. It is indeed real.

I am learning firsthand what the virus is all about. My only sister may someday become a statistic.

When I was working, I watched the news every morning while getting dressed for work. I once watched a segment dedicated to AIDS victims who had died and left family members behind. I think the show was aired during AIDS Awareness Month. The participants marched down the streets with red ribbons pinned to their chests.

In the middle of the broadcast, this huge quilt was displayed. Families were asked to design a patch to sew on the quilt in memory of their loved ones who had died from AIDS. Each family combined their patch with other patches. The quilt was large enough to cover an entire football field.

The patches are a reminder of AIDS destruction. AIDS reminds me of a racehorse storming to the finish. Anything getting in its' way will get crushed.

I watched the show with trembling legs. A sharp, sickening pain stabbed me in my stomach. The mothers talking to the interviewer expressed remorse for their dead child. The fathers and siblings added emotions. The broadcast did justice to the plight against AIDS.

Life is cruel. I pray I do not ever have to place my sister's patch on the AIDS quilt. I have faith; scientists will find a cure.

Scientists have been searching many years for a cure for the virus. Even before America was introduced to the virus in the late seventies, scientists were secretly working for the U.S. government. Their job was to do testing on select animals and humans. It was assumed a cure would be found before the epidemic affected America.

The AIDS epidemic was publicized extensively in the early eighties. The nation sounded the alarm. Certain nationalities were blamed more for spreading the virus. With time comes wisdom. We have since learned the AIDS virus affects us all.

Blaming groups of people for spreading

AIDS will not bring about a cure for those who are already infected. Pointing fingers will not bring victims back from the grave. Seriously, this is a national issue. This epidemic affects us all. Everybody is at risk!

I have heard people accuse homosexuals of spreading the virus. Why do humans always look for a scapegoat in every situation?

My response to comments made to humiliate others is to remind the person speaking that everyone is at risk. It does not matter if you are heterosexual, homosexual, or bi-sexual.

Gay people and lesbian people are not the only victims of this deadly virus. Where are the heterosexuals getting the virus from if they are not involved with homosexuals? This is a puzzling question. I know. What about the innocent babies? Old ladies contract the virus. What is the purpose of AIDS?

What protected me from contracting the virus? I do not know. I have practiced unsafe sex. I am not a drug user. I am not homosexual or bisexual. I have been with men who are high risk. Being young is not a valid excuse for making wrong choices. I am blessed to be AIDS-FREE.

Getting an AIDS test is not for me. I have gotten an AIDS test in the past. I don't think I would get an AIDS test today because I am frightened. I couldn't stand waiting for a week to get my results. I am not as patient anymore. I would rather die and not know I have the virus in my system. I could not live knowing I was HIV positive.

All of these thoughts about HIV and AIDS have a field day in my mind. Is there any place to hide? Will everyone become infected if a cure is not found? Will Desiree's remarks come true? Is she going to die from AIDS?

Chapter Fifteen

I think about AIDS every hour on the hour. I think about AIDS when I am in bed. I think about AIDS when I am in the shower. I think about AIDS when I am in class. AIDS is on my mind twenty-four hours a day even while I am sleeping.

I may appear to be strong or brave, but it is a shield. This is only a mask. On the inside, I am shattered glass. Many of us appear to be sturdy while wearing a mask to hide who we really are. On the inside, we are nothing more than cowards. We fear being vulnerable because this leaves us open to being hurt. We do not relate to another person's situation unless it has affected our life in some way.

There are those who make horrible statements about AIDS. Some say:

- "AIDS is a curse from God. He is warning the faggots."
- "AIDS was sent to get rid of drug addicts."
- "AIDS is a sign of the times. Jesus is coming back soon."

I get offended hearing people make any of the three statements. What makes them such an expert? Even the experts are not a hundred percent sure about the virus. Some people always have so much to say. They never close their mouth. I suggest all critics stop making assumptions about who started AIDS. You know what they say about people who make assumptions. They get in trouble.

I am guilty of adding fuel to the fiery furnace called gossip. I have ignited a few flames. I am guilty of gossiping about AIDS and where it originated. I intentionally made negative comments in the past not knowing my sister would someday become a victim of the virus. My behavior has backfired on me. I hurt so many people by my comments. A supervisor at my job was in tears from a comment I made about AIDS. She must know someone who has the virus. Someday, I am going to call her to apologize.

Before Desiree contracted the virus, I held negative beliefs about the virus. I have made comments about certain groups of people. I was wrong. I assumed I was right.

I was a self-proclaimed critic of AIDS victims. I thought I was an expert. I would make comments with no facts. I am sorry for all the harsh things I have ever said about contracting AIDS. What goes around comes around.

We never truly understand what a situation is like until it actually hits home. My lips are sealed. I am now walking in the shoes of shame. I have nothing else to say to demoralize AIDS victims. I now have firsthand experience with the virus.

My sister's situation has taught me some valuable lessons. First of all, I have learned to keep my mouth shut! Second of all, I have learned not to be judgmental (Judge Ye Not)! Third of all, I have learned to live each day like it is the last! Experience is the best teacher. Experience kicks butt. Experience has made me eat humble pie.

I am not a critic anymore. There are critics in

the world who have the exact attitude I use to have about the AIDS virus. Therefore, I do not expect everyone to have sympathy for my sister. Some people will say she got what she deserves. I will not talk about Desiree with anyone who is not a family member. They will more than likely criticize her lifestyle or think I have contracted the virus from my sister by hanging around her.

I use to have more than enough to say about AIDS. I use to have more than enough to say about everything. Patrick would beg me to be quiet. He always had to get on my case for getting in other people's business. I thought he was being the typical man, but now I know he was right.

To me, I thought we had the ideal family. I came from a two-parent home with a mother and a father. My parents always gave me whatever I wanted. Desiree and I dressed nice for school. Our parents treated us to dinner every Friday night. We had the picture perfect family. We lived in a glass house not realizing a single rock would shatter the windows.

Look at my family today. My mother and father are not living under the same roof. All of my friends from high school are married with children. I have nothing but a cheating man. And Desiree has HIV.

I was always offering advice. I thought I was perfect. As an adult, I was well-dressed, lived in a decent community, and had money in my pocket. I thought I was superior to women on welfare and Food Stamps. I called them lazy. I told a friend, "They can get a job. They have all of their body parts. Why can't they sell water on the street corner? They do not want to work."

I was wrong. I was not speaking from experience. I had no sympathy. I was saying whatever I could to make myself shine.

The tables have turned, and the script has flipped. Taxpayers are now wondering why I can't get a job. Why am I collecting their money?

As I have said in the past, "You can not understand another person's anguish until you have walked in their shoes."

I am on welfare. I also collect Food Stamps. I am not stable mentally. I cannot work. I am not handicap physically, yet I am handicap mentally. Depression is serious. It is more serious than I ever imagined.

Regardless of what the social workers think when I go to renew my file, I honestly believe I have earned the right to receive government assistance. I have worked ever since I was twelve-years-old. I was a newspaper girl not a newspaper boy.

I was the only girl who had a newspaper route. On Sunday, I delivered newspapers in my neighborhood. Although I was young, my mother wanted to teach me the value of a dollar bill.

I am on leave without pay from my job. My job is secure for one year. After one year, I can either return to work, or my position will be filled. They have hired someone to fill my position on a temporary basis until I make a final decision.

I should have enough years accumulated in the system to be entitled to government assistance and unemployment. I qualify for Medicaid. I cannot ask for Social Security or retirement benefits. I am not old enough. I have not applied for a disability check. I can apply pending a psychiatric evaluation. I would have to see a psychiatrist who would evaluate me, and make a recommendation.

All in all, I am at the lowest point in my life. "Ms. Miraculous" is actually human after all. I have the battle scars to prove I am human.

I use to go to the supermarket and grumble when welfare recipients were in front of me in the line. I rolled my eyes when they handed the cashier their Food Stamp Card. I made funny faces to the person standing behind me in the line. I complained about them having a shopping cart full of food.

Since the tables have turned, I am on the receiving end with a shopping cart full of food. I am loving every minute. The whispering voices in the grocery store line do not bother me. They can kiss where the sun does not shine.

The Food Stamp Program changed some years ago. Food Stamp Books are gone. Food Stamp Cards replaced the books. We do not have to stand in a line at the Food Stamp Office for hours anymore. They give us a card with money already deposited into the account, almost like an ATM card.

I go to the grocery store; select my food, and go to the register to pay. At the register, the cashier totals my food items and presses number ten on the cash register. The monitor responds by prompting me to slide my Food Stamp Card through the credit card machine. The regulations are the same for all purchases made with the Food Stamp Card. I am not allowed to buy personal items.

I wait for my AFDC Check to buy personal items. The money from the AFDC Check helps me with my bills. Patrick also helps pay my bills. I do not get manicures and pedicures anymore. I cannot afford the luxury. The last time I went shopping at the mall was when I was working. Why should I go to the mall anyway? What would I buy — a black dress?

Life has gone down the drain. When I was walking around with a three-hundred dollars purse on my shoulder, I was a diva. I was content. I was so content; I was selfish.

I had to sell my expensive purse. I sold it to a girl who lives in my apartment complex. Beggars can't be choosy. She gave me fifty dollars for my expensive purse.

My life has changed tremendously. I just did not imagine my life would be this way. I am reminded all the time of the things I did or said wrong to offend other people.

A man approached me on the sidewalk one day while I was heading to the Post Office. I ignored him. He asked me to spare money for food. I told him, "Get a job."

It is all so clear to me today. Most unemployed people do not work because they cannot function in a work environment. They prefer being somewhere away from the brown-nosing and harassment from someone who looks over their shoulder every second.

Something has happened in their lives forcing them to avoid society. It could have been the death of a loved one. It could be bullying at the worksite. The pressures of life got to heavy for them.

I met an older woman several years ago. She went from riches to rags. It all started after her mother died. She wanted to continue working, but it was impossible to be productive at work while carrying such a heavy burden.

She started drinking. Everyone was aware of her mood swings. She went to work drunk to cope. She thought her drinking was not noticeable. The smell of alcohol was on her breath whenever she arrived to work.

Her second trial came when she discovered her husband and daughter were having an affair. Her biological daughter was sleeping with her stepfather right under her nose. She never suspected a thing until she caught them for herself.

She left work early on a Tuesday. She went home to rest. Arriving at her house, she knew something was wrong. The way she tells the story is that the front door for the house was unlocked. She walked in thinking the house was being burglarized. She went upstairs to find her husband and daughter.

She heard a sound coming from the bathroom. It was the sound of the shower. She pushed the bathroom's door open expecting to find two dead bodies lying in a pool of blood. She found them there in the shower caressing. Her husband and daughter had just finished having sex. The stench of body fluids was everywhere. She looked down at the rug on the bathroom's floor. A circular spot rested near the shower. By looking closer, she recognized the spot to be a condom.

Soon after this incident, she lost her job. The boss fired her. She filed for a divorce. Her husband told the world she was crazy. Even her family believed him. He was so convincing.

She went to their pastor for guidance. The pastor turned her away. Her husband had already spoken to him. When she exposed the relationship between her daughter and husband to the church, they laughed at her. They thought she had lost her mind.

Eventually, her husband was able to get a warrant for her arrest. He accused her of attacking him. He claimed she was insane. Since her mother was dead, there was no one to speak on her behalf. The sheriff arrested her.

She spent ten months in a psychiatric hospital. Her family disowned her. I met this interesting lady while I was visiting my friend who is a nurse. I became her friend. I called her Ms. Crawford. This is her maiden name. Ms. Crawford did not want me to call her by her married name.

The hospital released Ms. Crawford after ten months. She immediately returned to her home. In the yard, she found a for sale sign. Her key did not fit the locks. Ms. Crawford did manage to break into her own house. Upstairs she found a douche bottle and feminine products in her daughter's bathroom.

Her husband had removed her clothes from the closet. Even her shoes were gone. She destroyed the house searching for her belongings.

Her husband arrived home that evening. She attacked him with a stick. Ms. Crawford managed to get in a few good blows before he knocked her out cold. She woke up to find him on the telephone calling the police. She did not want to be arrested again. She hurried to the front door, and rushed away from the house before he could catch her.

For weeks, she slept in the empty house across the street from her own house. At night, she would watch her house. Ms. Crawford had no money. She would sneak into her house after her husband went to work.

Ms. Crawford had to be cautious. She knew he had reported her to the police. The day came when she watched her husband pack all of her belongings on a Red Cross truck. He gave them her fur coat, shoes, under garments, and jewelry. He taped a sign to her belongings with a big smiley face on each bag.

This enraged Ms. Crawford. She lost her temper. She waited until the Red Cross truck drove away. Then she ran from the abandoned house. She ran straight for her husband who was standing on the lawn. He saw her coming and beat her unconscious.

Ms. Crawford was arrested for trespassing

and charged with assault and battery. The judge was going to give her four years in prison. Her attorney convinced the judge Ms. Crawford was temporarily insane.

As far as I know, Ms. Crawford is still locked away in a psychiatric hospital. I lost track of her. She was always so drugged when I went to visit. She didn't recognize me.

Ms. Crawford's story is true. I believed her although no one else believed her. Everyone was spreading rumors about Ms. Crawford all over town. They were calling her crazy. Ms. Crawford's husband has since remarried, and her daughter is attending college in another state.

Ms. Crawford's story proves life will eat you up and spit you out. Tragedy comes to us all. Even the richest woman can fall to her knees. We can never predict what we will do during a tragedy. Either you roll with the punches in life or you give in. The decision is yours.

It is my decision to stay here in bed all day. I can clean my house. I can go to a movie. I can do something productive. I choose not to move. I will stay here in bed, and wait for Sunday to disappear.

Chapter Sixteen

The lies associated with AIDS are deceptive. Even though people know they are infected with the virus, they will purposely infect someone else.

The silent drug user, the cheating husband, and the bisexual man in the closet are all forms of deceit, which eventually lead to destruction or AIDS. It is all about being honest.

If you are infected with the virus, be considerate of your partner. Do not intentionally spread the virus in search of revenge. You may know someone who you think deserves to die. It is not your choice. Man does not have the power to give life, nor does he have the right to take life. Before a person is born, their destiny is already written in stone by someone much greater than any man living in a fleshly body.

We all know what the result is of contracting the virus. Intentionally spreading the HIV virus is murder. The road leads to death. All those persons who have HIV and AIDS must learn to be forgiving.

Forgiveness includes forgiving the person who infected you. Make peace within yourself. Before the journey is resolved on this side, all feelings of hate have to be removed from the spirit so as to have a pure spirit when crossing over.

A man may meet a woman who is a "whore". In his mind, she is a "dog" who does not deserve respect. She has been around the block with all the fellows. Everybody calls her trash. Does this mean it would be right for a man infected with HIV to knowingly infect her? Think about her family. Think about her children. She may not be the most righteous person in the world. However, her family has a different perception of her.

There are kids everywhere wishing their mommy or daddy would come home. Infecting their parent with the virus would not only ruin one life but two, potentially more.

If you are already infected with HIV, why destroy someone else's life because of your mistakes?

How can anyone be so cold and malicious? The cycle has to stop somewhere. Desiree, for example, has two kids to leave behind if she dies. Not only does she have two children, they are young children. My sister has a family who will grieve for her. I will never get over losing a sister and a friend. My life would be altered forever.

We did not invite HIV into our lives. Robert did the honors. I think all HIV victims should not hurt others by spreading the virus. Every state should adopt some type of law to punish people who knowingly spread HIV. It is a crime!

I am frustrated with the world. I despise men. Why must men be so ruthless? Most men consider women like me to be bitter. These are the same men who cheat on their girlfriends and wives. These are the same men who have bisexual relationships.

The truth has to be told. It should be mandatory for all men everywhere to take a class on family, love, finances, respect, parenting, and religion. The money needed to fund these classes should come from the federal government.

I am sure the federal government can afford to fund an intervention program for men. These classes can be categorized with other assistance programs being offered by the federal government.

The purpose of these classes would be to assist men by offering counseling and education to improve life skills. A small incentive can be given to the men as a reward to encourage their participation. I think a certificate of some sort would be fitting to acknowledge completion.

Since I am on the topic of rehabilitating men, I might as well reveal how I feel about the way many men treat their women. Some women go through pure hell with their man. The men blame their behavior on their upbringing. They blame their upbringing on the society.

It is a shame when a man does not consider himself to be a real man unless he has three or four women. Don't they know having unprotected sex with all of those women spreads diseases?

Some men will go to any length to get what they want. I can't help but think about a man I dated several years ago. He was nothing more than a cartoon character. I am so glad he is not in my life anymore. He was a lying, sneaky, snake in the grass. He walked around pretending to be a Muslim. He knew the Quran like the back of his hand. He knew more about religion than a theology student at the university.

I later discovered his righteous talk was all a big scam. The topic of women revealed his weakness. He was dating me, another woman, and had a wife at home. I knew nothing about his wife when we started dating. He did not tell me he was married. I found out about his wife through the grapevine. A friend told a friend who told me. I confronted him.

"Don't worry about my wife. She knows about you. It is customary for Muslim men to have more than one wife. It has always been this way since the beginning of time," he assured me.

"You must be kidding me? I have never heard of such a thing. Marrying more than one woman is bigamy."

"No. It is not bigamy. You have been brainwashed by the system."

I asked him, "What system are you talking about?"

"All of the laws in America," he said.

"I know for a fact Muslim men do not have two, three or four wives." These words left my mouth while my head moved from side-to-side as I spoke.

"Says who?"

"Says me." I grumbled.

"I will take you to my wife. You can meet my second wife. You will be my third wife."

I laughed at him. "So you are telling me you went before a pastor and married two other women?"

"No. I married my first wife at the courthouse. I married my second wife at the Temple."

"So where would you marry me if our relationship gets to that point?"

"At the Temple," he responded with a great, big smile on his face.

"Why not go to the courthouse since you claim it is legal?"

"We have nothing to prove to America."

"Do you actually think I will stay with you after you have stood here and admitted to having a wife and a girlfriend? The second woman is a girlfriend not your wife because she is not legal. And your first wife needs to get her head checked," I told him.

I have heard about men having more than one wife. This happens in third world countries. In a third world country, a man gets to marry as many women as he can afford. We have different laws in America. A man who marries more than one woman in America will find himself in jail.

I have no compassion for men or women who have multiple sex partners. There is nothing wrong with having lots of friends just do not have sex with them. Be smart not horny. Friends with benefits is a way of fleeing commitment.

Women who allow men to abuse them carry some of the blame for the man's behavior. For instance, a woman may know a man is married or involved in a relationship. She will still allow him to enter her life. Even if his wife or girlfriend returns a message she left on his cellular phone, she vows to stay with him. Her values tell her to find a single man. Her heart tells her to wait on the man who is already taken.

My sister is the kind of woman who likes to defend a man. The man can be caught in the act of cheating, and my sister will make excuses for why he cheated or what his woman did wrong. My sister can catch her man cheating; she will switch the story in her mind to make herself believe he was innocent.

I have stood by my boyfriend when he has cheated. There comes a day when he has to be held accountable for his actions. Patrick knows I will argue until the cows come home. To prevent the headache, he sneaks around more than I would care to mention.

There is something else about women, which annoys me. We may know in advance a man is a womanizer. Something within us makes us think we will be the woman to tame him. From past experience, I know a woman is not capable of taming a man. If his mother did not teach him morals, you sure won't be able to convince him otherwise.

A man is intelligent. He will go along with the program until he gets what he wants from you or drains your bank account. Then he will leave you. Nagging will not bring him back to you. His mission will be accomplished.

Women must learn to love themselves and each other. We have to quit competing against each other for a man's affection.

Is this what life is all about — living to satisfy our

men? I recall a character from the Charlie Brown Cartoon asking a question. She would say, "What's it all about Charlie Brown?" I do not remember Charlie Brown's response. I only remember the question.

What is it all about? Do we live then die? Does anything ever occur in between all of the hardships to make us proud to have lived?

Life is unpredictable. Life is weird. Life is what I am regretting the most these days. I do not favor suicide although it seems to be the way to freedom. When stress grabs a hold of the soul, it plays on the heartstrings until the song becomes a faded heartbeat.

Billy Holiday knew all about the blues. Her life story reveals an autobiography of anguish. She was vulnerable to men. All of the men in her life were bad news. She tried drugs for the first time to please her lover. She did not know she would eventually become a drug addict. Her life was filled with misfortune.

Like many women, Billy Holiday was a sucker for handsome men. A handsome man could get Billy Holiday to spend all of her money. Her major troubles stemmed from bad relationships.

Billy Holiday sang songs about the blues. I love her music. Be it from another age, I can appreciate the words. My favorite tune by Billy Holiday is *Good Morning Heartache*.

I wonder if Billy Holiday had trouble getting to sleep at night. I, for one, can testify to not being able to fall asleep many nights. Going to sleep can be worse than getting caught in a thunderstorm.

On bad nights, falling asleep sends chills through my bones. I imagine myself sitting in a car with the windshield wipers moving fiercely from side to side as I drive through the storm. As I enter into the first stage of sleep, I close my eyes to see the rain pouring down. There is nothing I can do to make the ride easy. My defense mechanisms are useless while I sleep. It is as though demons ride my back all night long. I have nightmares about family members dying. I dream about babies drowning in bathtubs. I hear myself calling to strangers who have the voice of Satan. It is all so miserable for me.

Some nights are better than others. I sleep fairly well whenever my boyfriend is lying next to me. My nightmares tend to come whenever I am worried about Desiree. This is when falling asleep becomes a drive into a thunderstorm.

The deal with nightmares is how the mind has a way of playing tricks. I could remember my nightmares when they first started. After the nightmares began to come more frequently, my memory of them became very vague in the morning. Now I only remember bits and pieces from each nightmare.

I can always tell when I have had a nightmare the night before. It is written all over my face in the morning. My face looks tired, worried, and terrified. Another giveaway is my grouchy attitude.

Even sleeping pills do not help me very much. The sleeping pills make me drowsy. I do fall asleep. The nightmares still torture me throughout the night. The sleeping pills send me into a deep sleep where I have no control over waking up. It is almost like being buried alive.

I have been told to clear my mind before lying down at night. I have been told to pray before lying down at night. I have been told a ghost is in my apartment. And I should be nice to make it go away. I have been given many remedies except one that works.

Life sure is different since HIV came knocking!

Chapter Seventeen

I am determined to wear a condom from this day forth. I will even wear a condom with my husband. I have to protect myself. AIDS is real. It is about life and death.

There are an alarming amount of teenagers who have AIDS. Parents have to educate their teenager about sex instead of hiding the facts. It is okay to teach teenagers to say "NO", but we have to teach them what to do if they decide to say "YES". Do not make your teenager feel so ashamed of being sexually active until they skip school to be with a boyfriend or lie about going to a friend's house to be with a boyfriend.

Kids are having sex in elementary school. Sex is a trend. Having sex makes them popular. Education is the answer for teenagers and adults.

I was watching the late night news the other day when I heard about a ten-year-old girl who gave birth. I almost choked on my dinner. What does a ten-year-old know about sex? They are babies themselves.

My biggest fear is the rate at which this virus is spreading. If a cure is not found, this virus will kill half of America.

I hope Desiree is not in those numbers of people who die from AIDS. We should have known Desiree was sick. Because of our lack of knowledge about the virus, we were not familiar with HIV symptoms. The signs have been there for quite awhile with my sister.

Learning about HIV and AIDS can be complicated. The terminology is not clear. The words are big and hard to pronounce. It is a hassle asking around about the virus. Everyone has their own definition of the terms relating to HIV and AIDS.

I saw a pamphlet at Desiree's house. It read,

"HIV develops gradually by causing cells to mutate. Before HIV turns to AIDS, the immune system has a low T-cell count." I had to get a dictionary to define words such as mutate and T-cell.

I remember when Desiree started getting sick. This is before we discovered she was HIV positive. It was around seven-thirty pm in the evening. Desiree was rolling on the floor, complaining of stomach pains. The pains were excruciating. She could hardly move. She stayed there rolling on the floor and crying.

Desiree refused to go to the hospital. She thought her stomach would stop hurting on its own. The pain did not go away. The following day the pain got worse. Desiree had to see a doctor. She begged me to drive her to the Emergency Room.

We got to the Emergency Room. The nurse signed Desiree in. They did not make Desiree sit in the Waiting Room. The nurse could tell Desiree was in pain. I watched television in the Waiting Room while the Emergency Room doctor examined Desiree.

We stayed in the Emergency Room for more than six hours. Although I was exhausted, I refused to leave her there alone. Desiree came to the Waiting Room after being released.

I could tell she was feeling better. I did not ask her what treatment she received. She did not offer any information.

During the drive home, I wanted to know what the doctor had told Desiree. I asked her if I could see the release papers. She grunted and said, "No, the papers are in my purse. I would have to empty my purse to find them." I knew then Desiree wanted to keep the information private.

My sister was getting sick frequently. I lost count of the many visits we made to the Emergency Room. We were in the Emergency Room every week. Desiree was also visiting her doctor regularly.

I found some of Desiree's prescriptions from her doctor. She had thrown them in the garbage. I did not know what the medicine was for, so I put the prescriptions back in the garbage. I thought Desiree would have kept them if they were important. I never questioned her about the prescriptions unless she asked me for money.

Desiree was always borrowing money to pay the co-payment required to see a gynecologist. This reminds me. It is almost time for me to get my yearly pap smear.

All women are advised to have a gynecological exam once a year. I visit my gynecologist once a year. It has always been this way.

I will visit my gynecologist if I have a burning sensation, an itching sensation, or abnormal discharge. My gynecologist usually gives me some sort of cream or the Diflucan tablet to treat yeast infections.

I thought it was odd Desiree constantly went to visit her gynecologist. I know a gynecologist does pap smears, treats sexually transmitted diseases, prescribes birth control pills, and monitors for any irregularities in the vagina. Desiree did mention the results from a pap smear revealed she had abnormal cells. For the world of me, I could not understand why Desiree was always going to see her gynecologist. I was getting suspicious.

Desiree could not get rid of a yeast infection, so she claimed. With every day came a new feminine problem. Desiree got to the point where she was unable to wear underwear.

Her menstruation flowed very heavy. She had

to wear the really thick feminine pads given to women after they deliver a baby. Her bed sheets were getting stained from the heavy blood flow. The heavy flow of blood was destroying her clothes. Desiree told me she was having blood clots. I told her, "It is not normal for a woman to have blood clots all day during her cycle."

The blood clots got really bad. I took Desiree to the Emergency Room for treatment. I stayed in the Waiting Room until she was ready to go home. I was happy she got treatment.

My sister started getting a sore throat more than usual. I blamed her sore throat on the cigarette smoking and drinking alcohol. I told Desiree to get rid of the cigarettes. She refused. She thought smoking cigarettes maintained her weight.

Desiree does not smoke anymore. She hates the smell of cigarettes. They make her sick to her stomach.

Every now and then, Desiree has fever blisters in and around her mouth. Her many encounters with pneumonia causes the fever blisters. Whenever Desiree catches a cold, her temperature rises. This brings on a fever resulting in fever blisters.

An eye opening experience happened when Desiree was hospitalized for walking pneumonia. I then decided to watch her closely. The only way a person can catch pneumonia is when their immune system is abnormally low. I speculated Desiree was lying to me about her health.

Desiree was hospitalized for fourteen days. She was treated and sent home. She was so happy to leave the hospital. Her kids missed her. They wanted her home with them.

One month passed. Desiree was hospitalized again. She had walking pneumonia. I could not understand why she had walking pneumonia for a second time. In the early 1900's, people died from pneumonia because they could not afford proper treatment. In this day and age, people do not get pneumonia unless they have AIDS, are elderly, or have a terrible illness.

I mentioned to my mother, "Desiree should consider getting tested for HIV." Desiree was getting sick to frequently, and she had pneumonia.

My mother ignored me because she thought Desiree was not sleeping around with a lot of men. Desiree did not use drugs. She had never received a blood transfusion. She did not fit the profile of a person who contracted HIV. My mother did all the analyzing. She concluded Desiree was worried about finding a job. I accepted my mother's conclusion.

The days passed. Desiree was released from the hospital a second time. She went home in perfect health. She did not remain healthy. A visit to the doctor revealed she had high blood pressure. The doctor put her on a Low-Fat, Low-Sodium Diet. The doctor told Desiree to follow the diet until she lost twenty pounds. Desiree did not need high blood pressure medicine.

For every illness, Desiree had an answer. For every pain, Desiree had a prescription. For every yeast infection, Desiree took penicillin or something else. For her sore throat, Desiree reduced her cigarette smoking to eight cigarettes a day. She used ointments for the fever blisters in and around her mouth. There was always an excuse for every problem.

My sister was carrying the HIV virus in her system and did not know it. The doctors misdiagnosed her condition. Desiree assumed her body was responding to stress. I would joke with her about getting gray hair, but it was only a joke. She had not reached thirty. If stress was not causing her to get sick, what was?

Chest pains started. Desiree's doctor sent her to a specialist. The specialist had her admitted in the hospital for x-rays and a chest exam. Nothing was found. Her test results were normal. The doctor figured the chest pain was a result of stress. My sister was placed on bed rest.

Over and over again, Desiree got sick. Her doctor never considered testing for HIV. I believe many women experience the exact symptoms, and their doctor's never think to test for HIV.

Although Desiree was having her blood samples sent to the lab for review, they did not test for HIV. A patient has to sign a release form to be tested for HIV. The form is confidential and guarantees the patient's privacy. A doctor is not allowed to automatically test for the virus without consent from the patient.

I think all doctors should recommend a HIV test for all of their patients. Of course, this suggestion will offend some patients who are sensitive about the subject. There are patients who are afraid to get tested. Without knowing they have the HIV virus, a person can transmit the virus. Furthermore, no one would consider himself or herself at risk, which is why we fail to be tested. Being tested for the HIV virus is the only way to know where you stand.

The waiting period for the test results is enough to cause a migraine headache. Many doctors allow their patients to call in for blood work results over the telephone. The designated nurse can tell you whatever you want to know about the lab results; they can't tell you any information about test results for HIV and AIDS over the phone.

You have to schedule an appointment to see the doctor. In the meantime, you do not know if this means you have tested positive or negative. The pressure is unbelievable. The entire process of getting tested and getting the results makes a patient wish they had never been tested at all.

Desiree received many pamphlets from her doctor about *Living with HIV* once she tested positive. He should have given her those pamphlets before she tested positive. Maybe she would have protected herself.

CHAPTER EIGHTEEN

I glanced through some of the pamphlets given to Desiree. The pamphlets enlightened me in some aspects. I learned what symptoms we should have recognized with Desiree. I learned many things from the pamphlets.

HIV and AIDS are not the same. HIV causes AIDS. AIDS is the last stage of the virus. HIV is a virus. This virus weakens the immune system. This explains why Desiree had constant yeast infections. My sister had PCP which is pneumonia related to HIV. Another symptom Desiree had was Candidiasis commonly known as Thrush. White spots in the mouth are a side effect of Thrush.

HIV is also known as the Human Immunodeficiency Virus. The pamphlet I read states HIV can live in the body undetected for many years. My sister is fortunate. She knows who infected her. She knows when she was infected. Some people living with the virus do not realize it is "hiding" in their system. They then do not know who infected them once the virus is discovered.

The pamphlet I read discussed ways the HIV virus is transmitted. Body fluids including blood and semen are the main avenues to transmit the virus. I did not see any information about HIV being transmitted through teardrops. It did mention the HIV virus cannot be transmitted in the air, on toilet seats, or by touching someone's skin.

To my surprise, there are two separate tests used for HIV and AIDS. The HIV test detects antibodies related to the virus. The AIDS test is not administered if the HIV test is positive.

I use to have a phobia about hanging around anyone who is HIV positive. I thought being in the same room with a HIV patient would make me a candidate for the virus. This sounds stupid, but I was like many people — afraid!

The pamphlet discussed condoms. Latex condoms protect against HIV. Lambskin condoms do not. Condoms containing Nonoxynol-9 improves protection. Condoms are ninety-nine percent safe.

Desiree had a bag of condoms in her closet. She did not use them with Robert; she trusted him. She told me Robert refused to wear a condom. He told her sex doesn't feel the same while wearing a condom. He complained about condoms being too tight.

Men will refuse to wear a condom if the woman does not force him. Condoms come in all shapes, colors, sizes, and flavors. If one size is uncomfortable, he needs to find another condom to suit his needs.

I do not blame Robert totally for what happened to Desiree. She could have protected herself. All she had to do was stop for three seconds, and force him to put on a condom.

Women fall for the "I Don't Like Condoms Trick" everyday. Some women enjoy the moment without thinking of the consequences. Then some women get pregnant, get a sexually transmitted disease, or get infected with HIV. Sex can be a beautiful adventure if done in the right way, with protection.

You do not know what a person has done in the past. You only know what they tell you. By agreeing to have sex with one person, you have agreed to have sex with everyone they have been with in the past.

I was angry with Desiree. I wanted to know why she was so trusting. A bag of condoms was in her closet. All she had to do was use them. My mother warned her about Robert. Desiree knew he had multiple sex partners. She knew about the three or four "baby mamas".

Desiree is the reason why I have changed my life. I was angry because my own skeletons were coming out of the closet. Actually, I accused my sister of being to careless, but I had a secret lifestyle. She deserved to be chastised and so did I. We were both guilty of living a reckless life.

My anger has since turned into compassion. I have shared her tears. Desiree made a mistake. We all make mistakes. It would be wrong for me to hold this over her head. She did not ask to be infected.

Desiree has forced me to deal with the issue of AIDS. If it were my choice, I would probably still be ignoring HIV and AIDS.

Chapter Nineteen

With disgust, I think about my boyfriend. Why he cheats on me is a puzzle. Everything he wants, he was once able to get from me. He is treating me like I owe him something. Thank God I am falling out of love with him.

Initially, I was angry with Desiree for allowing Robert to infect her. I was so wrong for judging her. Here I am in a relationship with a man who cheats on me. I know he sleeps around. And I allow him to stay. I make excuses for him. I have managed to convince myself he is only here to pay my bills. In my heart, I know I am not being true to myself.

Patrick can infect me with the HIV virus. It can happen. I am not having sex with him presently. I am trying to teach him a lesson. It appears he is not listening, or my teaching techniques are not working. Because of my love for him, he could convince me to have unprotected sex with him. I would regret it later, but I would give in to make him love me.

I know I am weak for my boyfriend. Women he has slept with have confronted me. I defend him in their presence. I always cried later. I am not desperate; I am in-love.

By allowing my love for Patrick to govern my emotions, I am subjecting myself to whatever happens in our relationship.

Seeing Desiree and feeling ashamed of my situation, I am determined to get rid of my boyfriend. I have to think of a way to prevent us from having sex. I might ask him to get a HIV test. This will upset him. I know he will disagree to being tested. I will not argue with him. This will be my way of protecting me from the inevitable.

I sound like a confused woman. In some ways, I am confused. Why does love have to be so darn difficult? It is easy for me to fall in-love. Why can't it be just as easy to fall out of love?

Patrick is so smart. He knows I am tired of his cheating. Eventually, he will start behaving himself until the smoke clears. He will be with me every second of the day. He will shower me with gifts. He will do all of these things until I forget his cheating. He will go back to his old ways after I let down my guard. I know the routine. He has done this before.

Now that I think about it, even if he does change or agree to take the HIV test, our relationship is damaged beyond repair. The HIV virus can be hiding in his system for all I know. He is not worth me losing my life.

And to think, I stay home waiting for him. He has not asked me to marry him. He has not made a commitment to me. He starts an argument whenever I talk about marriage. He told me he is not ready for marriage.

I have to make the first step. The first step is ignoring his phone calls. The second step is asking him to return the key to my apartment. The third step is saying goodbye forever.

I thought the first step was not having sex with him. This does not amuse him. He has and will always have a woman on the side. The pamphlet I read about HIV and AIDS discusses oral sex and vaginal penetration. Patrick wants me to perform oral sex on him. I refuse. The pamphlet reveals oral sex is a way to transmit the virus. I did not know oral sex is dangerous.

Patrick dropped by on Monday night. He is such a liar. I listened to his many lies with a big smile on my face. What he doesn't know will hurt him. His days are numbered with me. He gave me a figurine. He always brings me gifts whenever he returns from a trip.

He told me he was exhausted from the trip. I was not concerned. He slept on the couch all night.

I suspected he would be there on Monday night. I went to bed early. I heard him open the door when he arrived. I made snoring sounds. He came in the bedroom, talked to me, and then went to sleep.

I smelt his cologne. The scent of his cologne remained in the bedroom after he went into the living room. In the middle of the night, I felt his hand on my shoulder. I knew what he wanted. I rolled over onto my stomach.

I ignored him. My body was motionless as he removed my gown and kissed my breast. I did not respond. I have told him how I feel about having sex with him. He thought seducing me while I slept would convince me to have sex with him. I proved him wrong.

Although my nipples were erect and I wanted him, I pushed him away. He did not want to take "no" for an answer. I had to think quickly.

He forced his way between my legs. Through his boxers, I could feel his penis. Fear sprinted around my heart. I was fearful of what came next. I rolled over and fell on the floor. I did it intentionally. I had to get away from him in a hurry. He spent the weekend in another state with another woman and expected me to have unprotected sex. For the first time in my life, I was afraid of a penis.

It is not easy watching my sister suffer with HIV. It is hard for me knowing she contracted the virus from unprotected sex. She had a choice. I have a choice. I am exercising my right to deny Patrick.

There is this red, flashing light in my head. It

is a warning sign. For me, the image of the red, flashing light keeps me grounded. I refuse to put my life in jeopardy. My mother couldn't handle losing both of her daughters.

I can prevent joining the list of people infected with HIV. The decision is mine. Do I want to live, or would I rather die? Any sane person would choose life.

Having unprotected sex is a death sentence. It is almost like planning your own funeral. I refuse to march into a situation, which will cost me my life. I am not going to do it for anyone including Patrick. He has to accept my decision. No more sex. I mean it! If he loves me, he will wait.

I intend to throw all of our sex toys in the garbage. The videos will go as well. No more sex. It is all over. There is more to a relationship than sex.

A condom can break. What about the area around the genitals? Genital warts are found in pubic hair. Condoms do not cover sores in the genital area. These sores can be quite contagious if they are leaking. I do not trust my boyfriend. Let the woman he cheats with accept him and his faults. Let her correct him, or risk dying for him.

I realize we have been very sexually active in our relationship. Intimacy is a big part of communicating in a relationship.

I think intimacy can only be satisfying when both persons love, trust, and respect each other. Patrick and I do not communicate about anything else in our relationship, so why should we communicate sexually? We can survive without sex. I know I can.

I may even become abstinent. This is my body. I am not obligated to do anything. He is not my husband. He is only a boyfriend. If I ever decide to be intimate with him in the future, it will be on my terms.

I regret giving my body to so many men for free. All they had to do was buy me a chicken dinner or a hamburger from McDonald's. My self-esteem was in the gutter. Men can smell a woman with low self-esteem from miles away. She is prey for them.

All the times I gave in for no apparent reason disturbs me now since I am older and wiser. I thought my body was only worth five dollars. That is how much a Value Meal costs from McDonald's.

Why did it take my sister getting HIV to make

me become a woman with high standards? None of the men who touched my body deserved me. Some of them acted as though they did me a favor – the nerve of them. I now know my body is a gift. It will not be traded in for a Whopper and large fries. I am somebody!

I use to have trouble saying "no" to a man. I thought all men were naturally sincere. I learned my lesson the hard way. I have no trouble saying "no" to a man today.

All men took advantage of me until I established my own identity. I had to learn to appreciate myself before I could expect men to respect me. Men can identify a woman who has low standards. Women with low standards are footstools for men.

I am proud of myself. I can actually be alone with any man on Earth and not have sex with him. He can be the cutest, finest man alive. I would still tell him "no". Besides, I am terrified of contracting HIV.

The fear of contracting HIV is way to heavy of a burden for me to bare. I could not live with HIV. I am not mentally stable enough to live with HIV. Life would be so miserable not knowing if I was going to die. I do not have a tremendous amount of faith in man and medicine. Man has not managed to find a cure for the HIV virus.

By Desiree contracting the HIV virus, it sent a big message to me. She has not given me a speech about being cautious. Watching her hurt has scared me straight. Desiree is my teacher. She is a basket case. She cries all day and sleeps when there are no more tears to be shed.

Desiree speaks of death everyday. I am sure there has to be more to HIV than death. For her, HIV is the conclusion of life.

Chapter Twenty

Sunday was a dreary day for me. Yesterday, Monday, was worse. I anticipate this week will be nothing to brag about. I have a class on Tuesday beginning at six-thirty p.m. This gives me the entire day to study, complete assignments, visit Desiree, or rest. I registered for the evening class to prevent having to be bombarded with work. The professors who teach the evening classes are more relaxed. Most of them are adjunct professors and only come at night to teach a course.

The adjunct professors are so much easier than the full-time professors teaching the morning courses. The professors teaching the morning courses are more geared towards the younger students who recently graduated from high school. The younger students are more in tune with studying and spending the entire day on campus. They are eager beavers. The older students are neither as eager nor motivated. Older students are burdened down with families, full-time jobs, and rent.

I am taking two classes during the day. I should have registered for all night classes. For the Winter Term, I will attend school at night.

Although today is Tuesday, I am not going to class tonight. My head is pounding. My body cannot stand to be in a classroom. I have to be in a place where I can move about freely.

It is five thirty-nine p.m. I use to watch the news at five thirty p.m. The news is not amusing at all. The news anchors appear to be falling asleep on the camera. Their job would be more exciting if they moved to the city where all of the action is happening.

Instead of watching the news, I will go to sleep. It is comforting to be cuddled in my bed. The serenity of sleep draws me near. It is quiet in my apartment. The loudest sound I hear is my own heartbeat. My heart is pumping blood faster than waves hit the shore. I am not concerned. My heart is in good condition. I have never had any illness involving my heart.

I am in my bed preparing for a journey into sleep land. Shortly after I get into bed, I fall asleep. I have a dream. In my dream, I am confronted by a group of cats. There has to be seven or more cats standing in a horizontal line. The cats are holding me captive in a room. The room is dark. I am pressed against a brick wall with my arms stretched to the north. The cats make no attempt to attack me. They only sit and wag their tails while watching me shiver.

My telephone is ringing. I wake up. The telephone is near my bed. I answer it to hear Desiree's voice.

"Shanna, are you sleeping?"

"Not really. What's up?"

"Nothing. Me and the kids wanted to know if you were at home."

"Why? Are you all coming over here?"

"We might swing by. Are you going to class tonight?"

"I am not going tonight. I will go on Thursday night."

"Are you going to be home for awhile?"

"I have no where to go."

"Can I bring the kids by?"

"Yes, have they eaten dinner?"

"Yes, they ate. I fried some chicken with mashed potatoes."

"If you have any leftovers, bring me a plate." I laugh.

"Okay. We'll be there soon."

Something has to be wrong. Desiree is leaving her house. This is incredible. What does she want to talk about?

I will stay here in bed until they arrive. I will hear them knock on the door.

I fall asleep. I can afford to rest until Desiree and the kids arrive. I want to have enough strength to hear whatever it is Desiree wants to discuss.

I sleep until I hear a knock at the door. I hear my nephew, Johnathan. I know it is Johnathan. I recognize his noises. Cleopatra knocks with both of her hands. She screams for me to open the door.

I get out of bed, and slip on my robe. I am

wearing my bra and underwear. I do not sleep in my bra at night. I do sleep in my bra during the day in case I have to get dressed quickly to go somewhere.

Before opening the door, I peak through the vertical blinds to be certain it is Johnathan. There is no such thing as being overly precautious. A robber can be anywhere waiting to do a home invasion.

While looking through the vertical blinds, I notice my sister standing behind Cleopatra and holding Johnathan. She has a strange smirk on her face. She wants to smile I can tell. Her forehead is filled with wrinkles from worrying.

I open the door. Johnathan stretches his arms for me to hold him. He is spoiled. Johnathan still drinks from a baby bottle. Everybody tells Desiree he is to big for a baby bottle. She needs to give him a sippy cup. Cleopatra strolls in with a precious grin on her face. Cleopatra is a delightful child. I will gladly adopt Cleopatra and her brother if my sister does die from AIDS.

"Cleopatra, get yourself a soda," I tell her.

"I am not thirsty."

"Are you hungry?" I ask her.

"No, we had pizza."

"I thought you all had fried chicken."

"We had chicken and pizza."

"Why didn't you bring your auntie a slice of pizza?"

"You didn't say you wanted a slice of pizza."

"You should have called me." I say with a smile.

"I will call you the next time we have pizza. Alright Auntie Shanna?"

"I am not hungry. I was joking around. Desiree, I thought you fried chicken."

"I did. Cleopatra wanted pizza, so I put a frozen pizza in the microwave for her. Me and Johnathan ate chicken and mashed potatoes."

Cleopatra sits down on the beanbag in the corner. Johnathan sits on my lap with his baby bottle in his hands. I take the baby bottle, and place it on the table. I do not allow him to eat or drink in the living room. He would ruin my furniture.

Cleopatra uses the remote control to switch channels on the television. She goes to Channel fifty-six. A comedy show is playing. It is a young person thing. I do not recognize the comedian.

Desiree and I go into my bedroom to talk.

We leave the kids in the living room. Cleopatra will eavesdrop if given the chance. Johnathan is focused on his baby bottle on the table. He is not aware of us leaving the room.

Inside my bedroom, we both lay across the bed. Johnathan crawls into the bedroom. He can walk with some stumbling.

"Johnathan, go with your sister?" I tell him.

"Cleopatra, bring me a soda, and come get your brother," Desiree tells her daughter.

I can almost guarantee Cleopatra told Johnathan to come in here. She wants to know what is going on. Johnathan gives his mother a frown and leaves with Cleopatra.

Desiree pops the soda and begins to sip on it. I can tell she does not like the flavor. I have to go grocery shopping. The only flavor soda I have in the apartment is Black Cherry.

"So, what's up? Have you been crying, Desiree?"

"I cried earlier; I am tired of crying."

"I know the feeling. I have never cried so much in my entire life."

"You don't have to cry for me, Shanna. This is my problem, not yours. You cannot stop living because of me. You have to move forward. If something was to happen to me, I want you to take care of my kids."

"Nothing is going to happen to you."

"Shanna, you never listen to me when I talk. My words go right in one ear and out the other."

"You're wrong. I hear you. I just don't accept what you are saying."

"Remember grandma use to say a person knows when it is their time to die? And I am telling you it is my time to die."

"You do not have the authority to determine when you will die."

"I had a dream. The dream came to me so clear. In the dream, I was floating on clouds. I could see my own funeral being held." Desiree appears lost.

"Please. Spare me. Dreams have no meaning. You have been thinking about death, so you would naturally dream about death. All of this is related to your subconscious thoughts."

"No, Shanna. I am serious! Listen to me! It is over for me. I cannot fight this anymore. I am tired of fighting. Life has been to rough for me. Why I have this virus is God's way of punishing me for all the wrong things I have done in my life."

"If that were the case, the whole world would be infected. I keep telling you to stop thinking negative. I have not been an angel myself."

"You do not have AIDS."

"You do not have AIDS. You have HIV."

"I have AIDS, Shanna. The virus has progressed in my system."

"Why are you saying this?"

"I went to the doctor several months ago. I have known since then."

"Why did you wait to tell me?"

"What difference does it make? You can't do anything."

"Desiree, please be quiet. I know you are angry with God. God punishes us in His own way. He can save you."

"It is to late for God to save me. Why did He have to punish me like this? Why is he taking me away from my kids?"

"Why not you? Why all the others who are infected? Do not question God?" I snap at Desiree.

"I am not questioning God. I only want an answer. I need to know why. He knows I have my kids to live for."

"What makes your situation different from the five children who lost their mother to AIDS? God loves us all equally."

"This is not love. Where is the love?" Desiree asks me.

"The years you have shared with your children are a testimony of God's Love. You could have been dead and gone, but God's Love has kept you here with us. You can live for many years with HIV or AIDS."

"The truth is to much for you to handle, Shanna. I am sitting here telling you what my doctor told me. It is my time to leave this place."

"Are you sick today? Did the doctor give you any information about your T-cell count? Why are you being a coward? We can make it through this together. You know I will do whatever I can to help you. There is nothing I will not do for you. What do you want me to do?"

"Shanna, promise me you will raise my kids. Pay special attention to Cleopatra. She is a girl. Girls require more attention than boys. Don't let my daughter get pregnant before she finishes school. Tell her the facts of life. Tell her about the dangers of having unprotected sex." Desiree lowers her head.

"I will teach her what I know, Desiree," I say this as tears roll down my face.

"Don't let Johnathan get involved with the wrong crowd. Johnathan is more of a follower than a leader. Shanna, try to marry a nice man. I want my boy to have a role model — somebody to imitate. And always remind my children of me. Let them know I made a mistake. Tell them I wanted to be here with them. You know what to tell them."

"You can tell them yourself. You will be here."

"And if I am not here, promise me you will love my kids like they are your own."

"I promise."

Desiree is not blinking her eyes. She is serious. I am crying. Why is my sister talking this way? She is not dying. It is to soon. I refuse to lose her. I am not ready.

Desiree has never been this sincere. How can she expect me to agree with her? She is not going to die. I refuse to throw in the towel. We may not be a rich family, but we can help Desiree buy some of her medicine. The medicine will prolong her life.

First HIV now AIDS. I think Desiree is telling a lie. She is depressed again. Her depression is making her talk this way. Just because a person has AIDS does not guarantee they are going to die.

A person can't be HIV positive one day and have AIDS the next. This can't be possible. How long was the HIV virus in Desiree's system? Why has it turned to AIDS? Is Desiree keeping something from me?

Whatever the night hides, it is gruesome. Whatever the day holds, it is unknown. This is a tragedy for my family. If I were an author who wrote a fairytale, it would go like this:

Once upon a time there lived a girl.
The girl's name was Desiree.
Desiree was such a trusting girl.
Her mother was afraid for Desiree.
Desiree trusted all the wrong people.
Her mother knew one day Desiree would regret being so trusting.
To protect Desiree from harm,
Her mother watched over her for twenty-one years.

Desiree became an adult and started to make her own decisions.

One day she met a man.

The man was nice.

He bought her gifts and flowers.

Desiree fell in-love.

The man was a wolf in sheep's clothing.

They had unprotected sex.

That was the end of the trusting little girl.

Chapter Twenty-One

It all seems so unreal. I listened to Desiree with my heart. I heard what she had to say. I watched her lips move to release every word. Her words are like worms eating my flesh. I am doing my best to stay positive.

I shake my head in disbelief. All of the plans we made for the future may never come true. Desiree's world is slipping away before my very eyes. She is not enthused anymore about our goals.

Desiree did not tell me she has AIDS. Why did she lie to us? Has she had full-blown AIDS since the day she told us about her health? I thought AIDS develops after the virus has lived in your body for several years. I am confused.

Desiree does not know how to continue with life. She has gone into a state of depression. I think our family would benefit from an AIDS support group. I will call the 1(800) number to ask for assistance.

I blame myself for not encouraging my sister to seek professional help. I should have found a counselor for all of us. Instead, I have joined the pity party. We are all pitiful. This includes my mother, my Desiree, and me.

When HIV and AIDS came into our lives, it destroyed us. Many families are experiencing the wrath of HIV and AIDS. And many families are like my family — in denial.

HIV and AIDS is the worst enemy my family has ever encountered. We are not prepared for this monster. Not knowing what to expect, and the element of surprise has left us defenseless.

The attitude held by my mother and I has caused Desiree to lie to us. Desiree has kept this secret due to fear. Maybe she thought we would not accept her. Desiree did not want to tell us she has full-blown AIDS. Maybe she thought we would turn on her.

When Desiree first told me she was HIV positive, I was frightened. I went to Desiree's house one day to visit her and the kids. I was going into the kitchen to get a drink of water. For a second, I forgot about Desiree's condition until I opened the refrigerator's door. When I saw the jug of water, doubt crossed my mind. I was afraid to use a cup at my sister's house. I was afraid to drink the water. I was afraid to use her bathroom. I was afraid to be close to her. I am sure Desiree could sense my fear.

Although my mind gave me many reasons to shun my sister, I did my best to be there for her in the beginning. I had to force myself to look beyond my own anxiety.

Desiree noticed the change in my behavior after confessing she tested positive. She told me, "Shanna, you can not get HIV by being around me. HIV is not in the air. You shouldn't be scared of me."

Those words from my sister play back in my mind today. I am ashamed. I was being more of a stranger than a friend. I allowed rumors established by society to dictate my actions.

My inconsiderate actions cross my mind regularly. Mistakes bury in the graveyard of my soul. I wish I could take it all back. I would do anything to take it all back. I did not mean any harm.

After our conversation, Desiree stands to her feet. She looks around in my bedroom. She smiles.

"We have had some good times. Haven't we?" Desiree asks me.

"We sure have."

"Well, I better get going. I will call you in the morning."

"Let's have breakfast. The kids will be in school."

"Call me. I will let you know then."

Desiree goes into the living room. She gathers the kids, and they leave. I sit down on the couch and call my mother. We talk about Desiree. I inform her about my conversation with Desiree. My mother tells me, "Let me call you later." I know she is upset.

I call my boyfriend next. His cellular phone rings twice. He answers.

"Hello," he answers.

"Hey, where are you?"

"I am on my way there."

"Guess what?"

"What now, Shanna?"

"I don't want any company tonight."

"What am I supposed to do?"

"I know you can find someone to get into. Sorry, I meant to say I know you will find something to get into."

"What is this all about?"

"Nothing. I want to be alone."

"I respect your decision. Don't make this a habit."

"And if I do?"

"You'll see."

"Goodnight. Call me tomorrow."

I slam the phone down. His threats don't bother me. I am going to get a peaceful sleep. He can sleep under the bridge for all I care.

I move the thermometer on the air conditioner to seventy degrees. I throw my robe on the floor in my bedroom. And I climb in bed. I am so hurt. I fall asleep with tears rolling down my face. Is this it for Desiree? Sometimes I wish I were never born. I really do.

CHAPTER TWENTY-TWO

Around midnight, I wake up from my sleep. My chest feels tight. I am wheezing for air. I sit up in the bed. There is a sharp pain in my chest. I breathe in slowly then release the air. I repeat this three times. I know I am not having a heart attack. I am to young.

I get out of bed to walk around. With every step I take, the pain lightens. I go to the bathroom cabinet to get some Mylanta to ease the discomfort. It has to be gas on my stomach. I open the bottle, and pour some of the liquid into the cap. I swallow it, and replace the cap on the bottle.

Before I can return the Mylanta to the cabinet,

my telephone begins to ring. My heart skips a beat. No one calls me at this hour unless it is an emergency. I place the Mylanta on the counter and hurry to answer the telephone. I have a telephone in the kitchen mounted to the wall. This telephone is nearest to the bathroom.

I answer the telephone only to hear deep breathing. It sounds like someone is struggling to breathe. "Hello. Who is this?" I say.

The deep breathing continues. "Hello. Who is this?" I repeat the same question again. The person is not saying anything. They are breathing very heavily. "Hello. Whoever you are say something." No one answers.

Suddenly, the caller disconnects. What is going on? Who can this be? My hands are shaking. Is it my mother? Is it Desiree? I have to know.

I check my Caller ID box. The last caller was Desiree. It is Desiree. I am light headed as I redial Desiree's number. The phone rings and rings. She is not answering. I hang up, and try again. She does not answer. I call 911. The operator answers.

"Police and fire rescue. Where is your emergency?"

"My sister is sick. She is at home."

"What is the address of your emergency ma'am?"

"She lives at 108 Glendale Road."

"Are you calling from 108 Glendale Road?"

"No. I'm at home."

"How do you know there is an emergency at this address?"

"I received a phone call. My sister was breathing heavy. She couldn't speak."

"Ma'am, does your sister have any children?"

"Yes, but they are never awake at this hour. Please get somebody over there. My sister is really sick. She has AIDS," my voice rises.

"Calm down. I am dispatching an officer as we speak."

"Thank you. I have to get to my sister."

I drop the telephone on the carpet. Where are my car keys? They have to be around here somewhere. I see them. They are on the coffee table. I get to the coffee table, grab my car keys, and put on my robe. I am not thinking straight.

The pulses on the side of my head are beating. My legs feel light almost as if I could fall to the floor. I exit the front door not forgetting to lock it behind me.

Outside, I run to my car. I have to click the box on my key ring to turn off the alarm and unlock the doors. Inside my car, I remove the club. Desiree I am coming!

The streetlights are blinking. The yellow caution light is showing. There are not many cars on the road. I do not bother to stop or even halt at the streetlight. Desiree needs me.

My car makes a roaring sound as the speedometer moves to eighty miles per hour. My sister needs me. I press my feet further down on the gas pedal. The speedometer moves to eighty-five miles per hour. My car is like a bird. It is flying across the roads.

Desiree is not very far from me. I will be there soon. I just realized I am not wearing any shoes. My feet feel hot against the gas pedal.

I roll down the window to catch some air. It is warm inside of my car. I proceed to speed across town until I reach the store on the corner. I have to make a left turn to reach Desiree's house. I swerve around the corner so fast my car almost flips over.

I hold the steering wheel to keep it steady. From a distance, I can see flashing lights. Those lights belong to the ambulance. They are parked in front of Desiree's house.

I slow down. Some police cars are here with the ambulance. I have to stay calm. This may be a false alarm.

I drive ahead in the darkened night to reach Desiree's house. There is nowhere for me to park. The ambulance and the police cars have the yard blocked. I park my car behind a police car. I turn the car off, and leave my car keys in the ignition with my car door open. I run to the yard.

The flashing lights reflect on the houses. Neighbors are standing in their doors watching, wondering what is going on. Cleopatra is not in sight. Johnathan is nowhere to be found. The front door leading inside of Desiree's house is open. Police are standing in the yard.

I walk pass the police to enter Desiree's house. As I enter the house, a police officer holds my arm. He prevents me from entering Desiree's bedroom.

I begin to cry and scream. I don't know this

man. Desiree needs me.

"Let me go. Where is my sister?"

"Hold on. Who are you?"

"I called the police. That's my sister in there."

"The paramedic team is working on her. Give them a chance to help your sister. You would only be in the way if you go in there now."

"I have to be with her. She tried to call me."

The police officer holds me. He won't let me go. I stand close to his body while resting my head on his uniform. He compassionately rubs me on the back as I cry on his shoulder.

Then I hear Cleopatra call for me. She is crying. Her fragile body occupies a space near her mother's bedroom.

"Come to me sweetheart. Come over here," I tell Cleopatra.

"My mommy is dead. Isn't she Auntie?"

I pull Cleopatra to me. "No, your mommy is not dead. Where is Jonathan?"

"He is next door. Ms. Rucker took him."

I stand here hugging Cleopatra and looking towards my sister's bedroom. The door is not closed. I can see a rescue worker pumping on her chest. There is an oxygen mask covering her nose. Desiree is wearing her favorite nightgown. She is lying on her back. Her arms are to her side. "One, two, three," the rescue worker counts as he pumps Desiree's chest.

The rescue workers are talking in the bedroom. I cannot understand what they are saying. A woman is injecting my sister's arm. They are all working so fast.

My chest collapses. A deep, shallow breath goes from my mouth. My saliva is beginning to accumulate. My mouth tastes funny. I hear bells ringing in my ears. They sound like bells on a cathedral.

I stand here waiting for my sister to get up and talk to me. I want to hear Desiree's voice. I have to hear Desiree's voice. The rescue team continues to work on Desiree's body. She is not responding.

For a second, I leave my body. I see the image of an angel soar from Desiree's room. The angel soars above Cleopatra and me. This is when I faint.

Someone places my body on the sofa in the living room. I was not unconscious for long. A police officer is rubbing a small, white container in front of my nose.

My first words are, "Where is Desiree?"

"She is in the bedroom," the officer answers.

"Is she alive? Is Desiree alive?"

The police officer ignores my question. I have to call my mother. She has to come over here. I ask Cleopatra to give me the telephone. She is sitting at the bottom of the sofa.

I wait for Cleopatra to bring me the telephone. The rescue workers are leaving Desiree's room. They are carrying their equipment with them. I still do not see Desiree. I am going to my sister. What can they do - arrest me?

I raise my body from the sofa. My robe is not tied very tight. My cleavage shows through the upper portion of the robe. I did not have time to dress properly.

"I have to see my sister. Will you take me to her?" I ask the police officer.

"Are you sure this is what you want to do?"

"Yes, I am sure. Take me to Desiree."

The police officer pulls me to my feet. He leads me to the bedroom. All of the rescue workers are gone except one who is wrapping cords to place in a box. Then I see the unimaginable. Desiree is on the bed. Her eyes are closed. Why isn't she moving?

Her body is stiff. It is lifeless. She is not speaking to me. Desiree would not treat me this way. Why isn't Desiree acknowledging me? Reality sets in. Desiree is gone. My sister is dead.

The rescue workers did not save my sister. Desiree is gone home. I cry and scream all at once.

My entire life is flashing before my very eyes. Playing jump rope with Desiree on the weekends as a child finds its' way into my memory. I would race to the medicine cabinet to get alcohol for our scraped knees whenever we got injured. For Desiree, I was her precious doll.

"Desiree. Desiree. I am here. Baby, open your eyes. I called the ambulance. I called them. I got here as soon as I could. Please Desiree. Come back. Don't leave me. I'm not ready. Please."

My sobbing fills the room. I hit my feet on the floor as I beg Desiree not to leave me. My nose is congested. I am having trouble breathing. My eyelashes are filled with tears. I can feel my tears rolling down my neck onto my throat and then to my chest. I shake my legs, wiggle my arms, and throw my hands upward.

The police officer attempts to pull me away from the bedroom. I resist. I go over to Desiree who is on the bed. I look at my sister. She is dead. I cry even harder. My hands cover my face. I am in total shock.

"Desiree, Oh God. Please." All I can keep saying is Desiree's name.

My lips are trembling. I am whimpering. The saliva is increasing in my mouth. I can feel it as I swallow.

"Oh God. No...."

I throw my body on Desiree. My head rests on her stomach. Her body is warm. I move my head to her chest to listen for a heartbeat. The heartbeat is gone. I place my index finger on her wrist to feel for a pulse. There is no pulse. I lift her eyelids to see if she is sleeping. Only the white part is visible. I cover my mouth in disbelief.

I watch on waiting for a miracle. Where is the angel? Save my sister. Bring Desiree back. I beat my head on the bed. I cannot feel anything. As I wipe my nose, stars flash in front of me. My eyes are all cluttered.

"Come on help me. Desiree is not dead," I tell the police officer.

"I am sorry. She is dead," he tells me.

I stand over Desiree's face to give her mouth-to-mouth resuscitation. I breathe into her mouth while holding her nose. I then go to her chest striking consistently. She is not responding.

After awhile, I discontinue CPR. It is not working. I sit at the top of the bed holding Desiree's head in my arms. I kiss her cheek, and whisper to her lifeless body.

"It is all over on this side. It is all over here. No more pain and suffering. You always wanted to know why life was so rough for you. It was your destiny. You were sent here to touch lives and make a difference. You have made a big difference in my life. I don't know how I will live without you. I will keep my promise. I will raise your children as my own. I promise."

Cleopatra knows her mommy is dead. She heard me screaming. I can hear her in the living room. She is saying, "Mommy, Mommy where are you?" This makes me cry even more. My sister, a mother, and a daughter has passed away. I will never forget this day as long as I live.

I have to leave this room. I regret leaving Desiree here alone. I walk away from the bedroom. I immediately go over to Cleopatra. She is now my daughter. I am now more to her than an aunt. My role is greater. I must set an example for her. I embrace my daughter in my arms.

CHAPTER TWENTY-THREE

Desiree is really dead. It all happened so suddenly. One minute we were in my bedroom talking. The next minute I was in her bedroom whispering to her spirit.

My sweet sister is gone. She left us all to soon. It doesn't seem right. I did not get the chance to say goodbye. I did not get the chance to heal old wounds. I did not get the chance to say, "I love you". In many ways, I failed Desiree.

I have to confront these unresolved issues in order to live productively, and raise my two children. I have to keep my promise to Desiree.

Now that Desiree is dead, I am reminded of the things I wanted to say but never got around to it. I was going to apologize for my behavior in the beginning when she told me she was HIV positive. I acted strange because I was not knowledgeable enough to know my sister could not transmit the virus through casual contact. I treated her like a total stranger.

Desiree and I had fights when we were kids. We are adults, but I still wanted to apologize for those fights. I wanted to clean the slate, to beg for her forgiveness. I wanted to correct all unfinished business.

I am burdened by these memories. I wish we could start all over from childhood. I want another chance! I want my sister.

This morning was the worst day of my entire life. I drove away from Desiree's house at two thirty-three a.m. Cleopatra and Johnathan were with me. I drove directly to my mother's house. She was in bed sleeping. I told her the bad news. She already knew. No one called her, so how did she know? I wanted to know how she knew my sister had died. She told me, "A mother has instincts."

I am now here in my apartment watching television and drinking a cup of coffee. It is eleven minutes after seven a.m. The kids are in my bedroom sleeping. I will let them sleep. I am not going to wake them. I will call my mother shortly to let her know we will be coming over there after the kids wake up.

I feel sorry for my mother. She has been in denial the entire time. My mother has to accept Desiree is dead.

Chapter Twenty-Four

A Rose is Not a Rose

As the dew drops roll down the gentle rose,
Trickling to the ground they go.
As the water sprinkles to the earth, they give life to the seeds in the dirt.
As the pain releases from your eyes,
faith comes with every tear you cry.
As the sun shines on the petals,
the rosebud opens to greet the meadows.
As Nature's grace remains in the stems,
it serves as nourishment for each of them.
As the day comes to an end, the beautiful rose lingers in the wind.
As the rose blows away, its' seeds have
been planted to bloom another day.

I wrote this poem for Desiree. I am not a poet. I wrote this poem as a tribute to my sister. I will read it at her funeral.

Even if no one else relates to the words in the poem, I am content because I lived the poem with Desiree. I am comparing Desiree to a rose. For me, she will always be a rose. A rose is still a rose regardless of the decay of time.

My last conversation with Desiree was in my apartment. I did not take her seriously. I thought she was talking about death due to her depression.

She left my apartment with a smile on her face. I think she was relieved. She was able to make arrangements for her children, which was her greatest concern.

The events of our last conversation replay in my head. I watched Desiree and the kids walk to the door before leaving. The kids were smiling. Desiree was happy to see them smiling.

My sister once told me she was contemplating killing herself and the kids. I know she loved her kids. They were her life. Her main concern about living with the virus was dying and leaving her kids behind. I think by me promising to be a good mother to her kids I made Desiree more accepting of what lay ahead.

My sister struggled half of her life. Her struggles were self-inflicted. She chose not to attend college. She chose not to marry her kids' father. She chose to allow men to misuse her. She chose her life.

She did not choose HIV or AIDS. The men my sister dated had one thing in mind—sex not stability. I think Desiree was worried about Cleopatra following in her footsteps. This is why she probably told me to give Cleopatra special attention.

Along with HIV and AIDS comes a high level of stress. Everyday brings new challenges. The days were all so strenuous dealing with Desiree. I now know that the stress caused by HIV and AIDS does more damage than the actual virus. It is a mental thing. Only the strong can survive HIV and AIDS. The virus has a way of promoting chaos wherever it goes.

I have not been to sleep since waking at midnight. I know I will have nightmares if I close my eyes. I am comfortable watching television. I have to be ready whenever the kids wake up. I have to console them.

Early this morning at Desiree's house, Cleopatra

wanted to call my mother. I had intended to call her, but I was in a state of shock. My mother would have arrived before Desiree's body was taken away. I know she would have wanted to see the body. It is best she was not there.

My mother did not want to shed a single tear when I told her about Desiree. She stood in her house looking around with glassy eyes. I thought she would cry. She was calm. I offered to stay with her. She told me she would be fine.

I come from a huge family. I have six uncles and three aunts. I am not certain how many cousins I have. My cousins have children. Then there are those who have married into my family. We can be found all over Louisville, Birmingham, Ohio, and Georgia.

More than half of my family will be at my mother's house today. Her sisters will stay with her for a few days. Her brothers will drop by to visit. My family will become even tighter during this ordeal. We all love Desiree.

My oldest aunt will organize the funeral arrangements; she works at a funeral home. She should know what has to be done. I am not in the right state of mind to do anything relating to a funeral. My mother is more than likely waiting for this all to disappear.

I sit here trying to watch the television. The sound from the characters is my comfort. Silence would drive me insane.

I was not born yesterday, but it is as though I am starting from scratch. I have not taken any parenting classes. I am unemployed. I live in a one-bedroom apartment. I am single. I have no potential husband waiting for me. I am a college student with nothing to offer children.

After the funeral, I will create a master plan for my life. I am not living for myself anymore. I have two lives to consider. They are most important.

Cleopatra is school age. Johnathan is not. I will put Johnathan in daycare. Cleopatra goes to Nightingale Elementary School. I can drop her to school on my way to work. I will have to return to work. Returning to work is not what I want to do. However, I have to support my children.

I will ask my cousin, Vivian, to clean Desiree's house. Everything has to be removed from the house. We can rent it to a married couple who has children. Their children will love playing in the big yard. Another option would be my moving into Desiree's house with Cleopatra and Johnathan. This is an option not worth considering. Living in the same house where Desiree died is a no-no.

The tenant who rents the house will be happy to find it is in a convenient location near schools and a shopping center. The grocery store is not to far away. The area is fairly quiet. And there has not been any crime in the area in all the years Desiree has lived there.

I have to decide what I will do with Cleopatra and Johnathan's belongings. I will go over to the house next week to let them collect whatever they would like to bring to my apartment. All of the furniture and anything belonging to Desiree will go to the Salvation Army. Who wants to keep those items around?

There is so much to be done. It is not necessary to speed to get all of this accomplished over night.

I wonder if Desiree is looking down on all of this. Psychics say a person's spirit lives on after they die. If Desiree is here in the room with me, I wish she would give me a sign.

Desiree was here yesterday. She is gone today. We spoke, and now she is dead. I can't communicate with her ever again. Even if I live until I am ninety-years-old, I will grieve for Desiree. Every thought of her will cause pain.

I am accustomed to visiting Desiree's house. From this point on, I will be dropping by Desiree's house to collect the rent from the new tenants. I will go to the graveyard to visit Desiree. This saddens me.

Imagine me kneeling down over a tombstone with flowers in my hand for Desiree. Would I actually be speaking to Desiree, or would I be speaking to a corpse? Is Desiree in heaven? Will she hear me?

I have gone to the graveyard before with a friend to visit her father. She placed a six-pack of Budweiser on his grave with a bowl of Doritos. I wanted to ask her what the food was for. To prevent offending her, I kept the question to myself. Her father will not drink the beer nor eat the Doritos. I guess the maintenance men throw those things in the garbage whenever they clean the cemetery.

I have a lot to do in the next month. Where I

will gain the strength to do it all is beyond me. My body is physically and mentally drained. I want to be in a bubble sheltered from the storm. I yearn to hear Desiree utter the words, "Everything will be fine, Shanna." Desiree said this to me many days when I was ready to quit and throw in the towel.

My true, best friend is gone. I will struggle to carry on. I will cry for Desiree for evermore. On her tombstone, there will be the words *My Beloved Sister*. Although her body will be in the ground, the layers of dirt won't keep her from me. She lives in my heart.

CHAPTER TWENTY-FIVE

I move from the couch to sit on the floor. I finish drinking my coffee, and place the cup on the dinette table. I drank an entire cup of black coffee. I have never drunk an entire cup of black coffee before.

My body is uneasy, but I am not sleepy. Cleopatra and Johnathan are in the bedroom sleeping. They need to rest. I have to make their breakfast. I am not a good cook. I will give them a bowl of cereal to eat until lunchtime.

My eyes are scratchy. My eyelids are heavy. The area beneath my eyes is puffy.

My nostrils are inflamed. My nose is congested.

I accept what is happening in my body as I stretch my legs on the rug.

I use the remote control to switch channels. Television stations cater to the younger generation more than any group. All of the shows are geared towards exercise, music videos, and cartoons.

Finally, I stop to watch Channel Six News. I wonder if it will rain today. The morning team usually gives the weather broadcast for the day. After I hear the weather broadcast, I will switch over to Channel Four News to hear about current events in the community. I have nothing else to watch.

A familiar news broadcaster stands in the middle of my television screen announcing the weather. He says, "There are some clouds over the Midwest. Today, we can expect sun at a high of ninety-two degrees."

Heat. It is going to be hot today. This makes me think about Hell. Is it hot down there? I believe Desiree made peace with her Higher Power. There is no way she went to Hell. This is a useless thought. This thought does not deserve to exist.

I sit here wanting to escape my own body. I want to suspend my body in the air, to drift easily down tranquility lane. This is the place for me, a place where no more crying exists. And in this place, I will be with my hero - Desiree.

These ideas simmer. Is there such a place? While asking myself this question, I hear a key being inserted in my door. It has to be Patrick. He should have called me before he decided to come over. He is not welcome here anymore.

I wait for him to come inside. He opens the door to find me sitting on the floor watching television.

"Shanna, why are you up so early? I was going to surprise you."

"Please. Save your surprises for another day."

"I know you want me to leave. Let me say what I came here to say. After that, if you want me to leave, I will go."

"Come in, and close the door." I snap at him with a stern voice.

He follows my instructions. "Shanna, I love you. I loved you since the day I laid eyes on you. I have not been faithful to you. I have done wrong. I accept my faults. Our relationship can't get any worse. You have turned against me. I blame myself. I am asking you to forgive me. Give me another chance. You know I love you."

"Is that all you have to say? I have heard it all before. You asked me to listen. I did. Do you have anything else to say? Your whining is boring me. Why don't you do this? Leave my key, and get out of my house!"

"Shanna, you have not heard this before."

I laugh hysterically. "As I said, leave the key, and get out!"

"Before I leave, I have one last thing to say."

"Hurry up. You are wasting my time."

He comes close to me and gets down on his knees. "Will you marry me?" He removes a black box from the pocket on his blue jacket.

"Will I what?"

"You heard me. Will you marry me?"

"Marry you. Why would I marry you? You would cheat on me with every woman in town."

"Shanna, I have never been this serious in my entire life. I want you to be my wife. I am not perfect. I can assure you my cheating is a thing of the past. Let me prove myself. You don't have to marry me right away. We can wait until you are ready. What I am trying to say is I'm not getting any younger. I am ready to settle down. I want it to be with you. I am begging you to give me another chance."

He is not joking. He has a diamond engagement ring flashing in my face. I wanted to marry him. I am skeptical of him. He has hurt me too much.

I am now a mother with two children. A father is a necessity. I promised Desiree I would take care of her children. Johnathan needs a role model. I will not be able to teach Johnathan how to be a man. Only a man can teach him masculine things. I am in no position to do this by myself.

Marrying Patrick will provide a steady income. He has a sensible paying job. He has health insurance with benefits. The kids will need all of these things and more.

I have to remember I am not in this for myself anymore. I have Cleopatra and Johnathan to consider. I admit I am not in-love with Patrick. Still, I do love him. He can make me fall in-love with him again by treating me right. For the sake of the children, I extend my arm to Patrick. He places the ring on my finger. Then he stands to his feet to hug me.

I have a history with Patrick. I know how he thinks. I would be better off dealing with him rather than starting over with someone new. I have a daughter to think about. I cannot have a lot of men coming in-and-out of my life. I have to set an example for Cleopatra. Patrick has the potential to be a good husband. He came from a good family. I guess he needed to grow-up before deciding to settle down.

"Yes, I will marry you."

"Thank you, Shanna. I love you."

"I have something to tell you."

"What?"

"Desiree is dead."

"When?"

"Early this morning."

"Why didn't you call me?"

"I was not going to call you anymore."

"So you were going to walk away?"

"Yes, I was going to walk away and never look back again. I can't play these games with you anymore. I hope you know I will be raising Cleopatra and Johnathan. I promised Desiree I would be a mother to them. If you want to marry me, you will be getting me and two children. It is a package deal."

"That's alright with me. You don't have any children of your own. I don't have any children of my own. This is perfect. We have a ready-made family."

Patrick's comment touched my heart. He is willing to accept me and two children. There aren't many men who will agree to raise someone else's kids. Desiree would be so proud of me.

"This was meant to be. Your sister's life is over. Our life is beginning."

"What are you talking about? I wouldn't trade my sister for you!"

"Calm down, Shanna. I can never replace Desiree. I am only saying Desiree would be proud of us."

"You're right. She told me to find a nice man to marry."

"I am a nice man. I made some wrong decisions, but I am a nice man."

"I know you are."

I have to weigh and balance my options. Patrick is not my husband. Technically, he does not have to commit himself to me. There is no law in America requiring a boyfriend to remain devoted to his girlfriend.

A man knows when he is ready to settle down. He cannot be forced into marriage. It has to grow on him.

Everybody deserves forgiveness. We all make mistakes. If I do not forgive Patrick, why should all those people I hurt in the past forgive me? Desiree forgave me.

Chapter Twenty-Six

There have been days when I had no struggles in my life, but I did not appreciate those days. I always found an excuse to complain. Some people are like me. We complain no matter what happens. We never take time to be thankful for what we already have.

Dealing with Desiree, HIV and AIDS is the biggest battle I have ever confronted. I thought my small problems were worth worrying about. Now, I have been confronted with a huge problem. And I realize all the times I spent crying over a bad grade in class or complaining about not having the right color pantyhose were small issues.

HIV and AIDS give no rules. It is not like playing

a board game were the instructions come in the box along with the game. With HIV and AIDS, you learn as you experience the everyday complications.

My mother and I allowed our emotions to overwhelm us. We stopped functioning in life, so how was Desiree going to function when her support system was weak? I think Desiree's boyfriend was more understanding than everyone else.

No one knows what it is like having a family member who has HIV or AIDS unless they actually experience it firsthand. There is more to the virus than getting sick. Along with the virus come financial burdens, isolation, depression, and loneliness. It is like being pushed over a cliff not knowing if you will land on rocks or in a raging river.

In Desiree's defense, I have to profess there is nothing wrong with falling in-love. Loving another human being is not a crime although it is a crime to love someone else more than you love yourself. Desiree loved her men more than she loved herself. When a woman loves a man more than she loves herself, she is like Desiree: blind and willing to do whatever it takes to keep him satisfied.

I want so desperately to mend what has happened

in our family. I think HIV and AIDS is a wake-up call. My family will never be able to forget the horrors of this virus. We have lost Desiree.

There is not a family alive who will not be touched by HIV and AIDS. When their time comes, I wonder what they will do. I wonder if they will hide from the truth. I wonder if they will disown their relative.

You may think HIV and AIDS will never touch your family, but I promise you it is coming. If you do not know someone who has HIV or AIDS today, believe me it is best to prepare yourself. This virus will kill millions of people. Every family should become educated about the virus. It is better to be prepared in advance than to wait until you are forced to learn. My family was not prepared. We did not know how to help Desiree.

Shame, guilt, and fear are the three biggest side effects of HIV and AIDS. I have learned that HIV and AIDS is not an uncommon virus. People who have the virus are not aliens. They have the same needs as everyone else. They did not ask to be infected.

If I ever get enough courage, I may consider becoming a spokesperson for AIDS. I think there are so many people alive who are still blindfolded. A person like me could help them realize HIV and AIDS is silent, but it is also deadly.

I would make my message available to anyone who wants to listen. I have no plans to discuss Desiree in the beginning. I am not ready to tell everyone my only sister died from AIDS. I have a long way to go before I am healed myself. My healing process will come gradually as I put the broken pieces back together.

I am alive for a reason. I wanted to die with Desiree, but who would take care of my mother, Cleopatra, and Johnathan? All of us have a calling in life. I think I just stumbled upon my calling.

From this point on, I will raise my children, take care of my mother, be a worthy wife, and become an advocate for AIDS. I may even change my major to pre-med. Instead of blaming scientists for not finding a cure for AIDS, I can become a part of the solution.

I can work along with scientists to find a cure for AIDS. If I were to become a scientist, I will be the first scientist in my family. And who knows? I may just be the first female, scientist to find a cure for AIDS.